CO-INCIDENTAL ENCOUNTERS

THE ROOT OF IT ALL: BOOK TWO

T. XORÌ WILLIAMS

FOR MY ONE AND ONLY. MY BEST FRIEND. MOM,
I LOVE YOU!

ACKNOWLEDGMENTS

I would like to express my love and gratitude to many people who saw me through this book. To everyone who provided support, discussed topics, read, and commented. Thank you all so much.

Above all, I would like to thank my number one fan, my mother: Margaret Williams, my rock and my best friend. Your strength gives me continuous courage. We've gone through many hardships, but you never complained nor gave up. Instead, you've learned to endure the hard times and raised your children to be just as humble as you are. I attribute all of my success to you. Thank you for always providing your never-ending support and encouragement. I have no clue where I'd be without your love, support, and dedication. Please continue to be strong! I love you for my life!

My one and only savior, my God. Thank you for seeing me through the best and worst times in my life. Continue to keep us in your prayers.

My second biggest fan! Karen Langford! Thank you so much for reading book one, *Co-Incidental Encounters Unbearable,* the moment it hit the shelves! I am sure you'll do the same with this book! Thank you always for your support and for being such a great friend!

Thank you Lisa Dietz for your ongoing support.

Laurine Deans, aka Aunt Hazel!! Thank you so much for your encouragement and for enjoying the book! Your feedback meant to the world me, thank you so much! I love you.

To the rest of my family, I love you all…

To my twin brother Barry, aka B-Wise! Thank you so much for your support and for sharing my book at any opportunity you got! My fanbase grew bigger because of you! Many people understand the importance of sharing content and yet they do not share; however, you did! You are my world, thank you!! Big Sister Tasha, who supported and encouraged me! You too are my world. I love you both endlessly!

To my second brother Rah… Aka Dun Dun… Thank you so much for all of your support! Love you, Dunny!

160 family, I love you all, thanks for the shares and love! Much respect for that!

Our angels Fat Sha, Uncle Wize, Sha blood/pretty Sha, Gregory Finch, Cory Tuner, Kirk Wilson, Shevonne Decamp, Uvalyn Chisholm aka aunt Una, continue watching over us all. May eternal rest be granted unto them, and let perpetual light shine upon them. May the souls of the faithful departed, through the mercy of God, rest in peace.

Last and not least: I beg forgiveness of all those who have been with me over the course of the years and whose names I have failed to mention. I love you all!

Clearing out the clutter in our lives, physically and emotionally, helps to strengthen the flow of our energy. Forgiveness, love, and peace greatly enhance our energetic health. Reiki helps to strengthen the body's energetic flow to bring back balance and promotes well-being on all levels. Energy centers throughout the body to receive and transmit energy messages. Our bodies are pathways for energy to flow. Root, Sacral, Solar Plexus, Heart, Throat, Third-Eye, and Crown. Please note that strengthening and unblocking your Chakras will create peace! #mybodymatter

Rain cascades down the windows of my car; the sun is rising, and the view is resplendent. I've been parked outside of his home for nearly two hours, contemplating why I overreacted last night. I know he's completely into me; however, I'm extremely nervous about advancing to the next level. Most men I've come across always change after the *first time*. The sound of the rain hitting the car makes each minute feel like an eternity. Anxiety has overcome me; my nerves have become uncontrollable. Thoughts of him dance across my mind. I can't take it anymore. I turn the car off and emerge into the rain shower with no umbrella, slowly jogging to the front door. I just need to see his face, and hopefully, he will forgive me.

"Hi, did I disturb you?" is all I can muster.

He looks at me soul-deep, then turns to walk away, leaving the door open for me to enter.

I follow, admiring his athletic frame.

"I just came by to say it was foolish of me to react the way I did last night."

He continues to walk to the kitchen in silence.

"Are you going to say something.... anything? I'm apologizing." Reaching the counter, he turns around with a cup of coffee and hands it to me.

"The good men always get the rough end of the stick." Although he is similar to some, he is absolutely more convincing, and his words pierce so deep with warmth.

"Now you were saying?" are the last words I hear before he presses against me. He takes my free hand and places it on his shoulder; simultaneously, he removes the cup of coffee from the other.

He places my hand in his, and we interlock fingers. Our eyes are glued to each other as he lifts me onto the granite-covered island; he is now standing between my legs, running his fingers across my collarbone. Every hair on my body stands up as chills shoot through me like electricity. I display an open smile, and attempting to take control, I trace my thumb along the edge of his boxer briefs. He looks at me, confused; I slowly reveal the back stem of his penis until it is entirely exposed. I

2

slide down off the countertop, and our eyes follow as I go down to please him. I begin to probe his penis with my tongue. I twirl and curl with each motion, glancing at him. His eyes are closed as he enjoys the moment.

He raises me once more and lays me across the kitchen island. My sundress presents easy access to my sweet nectar. I watch him take control. I begin to pull on my nipples, arching my lower back off the counter. He kisses the lips of my vagina very passionately, performing harmonizing movement between his tongue and finger. The intense heat of him against my eager pussy lips is hot enough to burn coal. As he continues to tease me, I am now soaking wet, and all I know is I want this man, and I want him now.

I place my hands on his head, pushing my hips forward.

"Ooouuu God," I whisper. He lifts his head, and we look far into each other's eyes. I then use both hands to place a condom on, then guide his love muscle into me. All of his huge penis thrusts so deep in me, I felt it nudge my back walls, causing pressure against my stomach. I clench my walls around the shaft to hold it in the same position. I can sense he's fighting hard to hold back. He tries to spread my legs, but I kept them tightly wrapped around him as his thick dick pulls my clit, rubbing it in rhythm each time he thrusts. I rotate my hips side to side, up and down. He is stretching me to the limit, but this beautiful pain is rippling through my body.

"God, you feel so good," he says.

I then cry loudly throughout my clenched teeth. I can feel the buildup between us as I dig my nails into his back, my legs wrapped around him tightly. Our moans are becoming louder and shallower. My eyes are squeezed shut. I want to hold back and wait for him, but I can't. My pussy creates a tightening spasm, and we conclude one massive climax together. Our bodies are quivering against each other, his dreamy eyes staring at me.

"You are full of many surprises, Zamora."

"I want to express that I haven't felt this way in such a long time; I've concealed all feelings toward men. Yet since meeting you, all of my endorphins came alive. I will try to curb my fears and relish this moment. Just promise me one thing, Oscar, promise me you will not hurt me…"

CHAPTER ONE

TRYING TO HOLD ON

As I stare at my husband tossing and turning from his night terrors, I often wish there was more I could do to help with his pain. Losing his boxing career was a traumatic experience for him. Well, for both of us, actually.

Even though it's been quite some time since the incident, I still feel as if I am failing helplessly with supporting him. I also feel as if I am detached from my husband. At one point in our marriage, we were glued at the hip, spending much of our time with each other. We used to do so much together, like getaway trips, family outings, picnics, making love all day long, dancing, night strolls. Staying up all night just conversing about anything that came to mind, whatever you could think of, we did. But at this time, we are passing ships in the night. I am lonely and concerned that I am losing my husband.

Suddenly, he wakes up screaming from his night terrors, and as usual, I cradle him back to sleep. Several hours later, I plant a few kisses on his chest, indicating I want to make love. Sadly, as usual, I just get, *"Not tonight Zadie,"* and he turns his back to me... Welp, into the bathroom I go with my vibrator.

I couldn't fall back to sleep, I was over the edge with thoughts running through my mind, so I decided to try and sleep on the sofa. Upon rising, I hear footsteps in the distance.

"Baby Z, why did you sleep on the sofa? Is everything okay?"

I was crying all night; my eyes are so puffy...

"What's wrong, baby?" Nazzir asks as he walks into the living area where I lodged myself after my emotional roller-coaster last night.

"Naz, I don't know what else to do about us..."

"No, no, no, I am not with the running lips this morning, Zadie. Call your sister."

I am abruptly cut off mid-conversation. "Why can't you just listen to me? I am losing myself, Naz; it has been months since you've touched me, months since you've told me that you love me. What else do you want me to do, not talk about my feelings?!"

He walks toward me. "Zadie…" he says as he leans over and plants soft kisses on my forehead, grabs my hands, and takes a seat next to me. *"Baby, you know that I love you with every beat. I was thinking maybe I need to see my therapist again; it's been a while, and I feel as if it is time again. I will try my best to fix this. Tell me what you need me to do, and I'll do it..."*

His eyes say it all as he sits beside me. There is the man I fell in love with, the compassionate, loving, sweet man I once knew. I am unable to hold back tears. In moments I've succumbed to my weakness and go into a bawling fit.

"NAZZIR, this is it. This is what I need from you: your positive energy, your passion, and your love. I can't live without you. I just wish you were this proactive a long time ago. I lost myself, Naz, I lost myself in you, in your pain, and in your doubt. I felt your negative energy, the elephant in the room, the space that was wedged between us while we slept. I need love, not only a friend but my husband. I am not trying to put this relationship on the line, but I am just expressing my feelings."

During my venting, Nazzir places the most passionate kiss on my lips and gazes into my eyes.

"You are everything to me, Zadie, my earth, my life, and I'll do whatever it takes to make you happy. I refuse to be without you. I will conquer all that we need to get back on top. Give me your hand."

I reach my hand out as he focuses deep into my eyes. We begin kissing.

"I am so sorry I kept you in turmoil."

"Baby, stop talking." I grab his hands and lead him into the bedroom. Lights dimmed, he presses his chest against mine, grabs my waist, then positions me in the center of the bed. We remove each other's clothes. He opens my legs, kissing in between my thighs, leading toward my beauty. Naz indulges on my pussy as if his life depends on it; he begins sucking and softly biting my clit while blowing on it at the same time. I grab the back of this neck, moaning softly, and whisper, "I love you so much; I never want to lose you."

He gently squeezes both breasts while sucking and softly nibbling on my nipples. "I don't want to lose you either." While our eyes are still connected, he slowly goes back in between my thighs to finish what he started. His tongue is swerving vigorously over my clit as he inserts his tongue, then fingers, then his tongue again, mouth-fucking me over and over again. My legs begin to tense, my toes begin to curl, and my waist is lifted while grabbing the back of his neck. I cry because I haven't felt this intense pleasure in a while.

"Nazzir, baby, please don't stop, please don't." Before I know it, I am screaming at the top of my lungs, but he keeps going. My thighs tense up so forcibly, I think I've suffocated him! He comes up toward me with my nectar all over his beard, and I grab him and lick my secretions off his face. Within a few minutes, I am knocked out.

The last thing I remember is Naz whispering in my ear, "Love you, baby, get some sleep."

The sound of his voice puts me at ease. Naz's love for me at one time was unwavering; I just want that back.

CHAPTER TWO

The following morning, things are back to what I remember. We are just sitting next to one another, eating breakfast, laughing, and watching the morning news. It's Saturday morning, and we usually go our separate ways. However, this morning, we decided to make this day about us.

He served me breakfast; we took a shower together, we laughed, we cried, and we talked for hours.

Since the summer is just about over, we agreed to take advantage of the sunshine and go someplace beautiful. So we decide to take a local one-day trip to Shelter Island for a truly relaxing vibe. The island is only available by ferry, and as we all know, there's something about sightseeing from a ferry that you just can't beat. The island is an intimate retreat with pristine beaches and a tranquil breeze. Our time turns out to be an accumulation of full days and sexual nights. We have an amazing time together, just two children foolishly in love. We are finally one—finally.

Sisters:

It is past nine in the morning when I make it out of the Hamptons on my way to link up with my sister Zamora at her dance studio for a lunch date.

Sitting in my BMW, I glance at my watch; it is slightly past 11 am. Zamora comes out several minutes later and joins me in my car.

"Hey, sis, you looking good!" I say, smiling from ear to ear. Zamora is always in perfect shape, 5'7 with an athletic build but still curvalicious, with rounded buttocks and toned legs. Her brown hair is twisted up into a ponytail. Even though she is wearing a sweatsuit, she is still shining, sassy, and sexy. Moments later she looks at me, rolls her eyes, and snaps her neck.

"Girl, I am tired and sweaty in this outfit, ain't nothing good looking about me at this time."

We chuckle. We are now en route to the restaurant. At one point, I thought my sister was a lesbian—not saying there's anything wrong with that, but she never dates.

She is just all about work, her girls, and me. Even though I know this is a sensitive subject, I just have to ask....

"So, sis, are you dating yet?" My heart drops, awaiting her response.

"Yes, I am actually."

I am fucking stoked! "No damn way!! Who is he, where is he from, what does he do, when can I meet him, does he have any children, spill the fucking beans!" As excited as I am, I damn near almost kill us by driving off the road.

"His name, his name is Timmy the bob, aka my dildo." No, this bitch didn't! I am staring so long at this green light in awe as cars honk at me to move.

"Seriously, Zamora?"

"Oh my, you should've seen your face, it was the funniest thing ever!" If I wasn't driving, I would give her a look to kill!

"That was really foul, sis, dead foul, but okay, I got you. I was so excited you were finally talking to someone, preferably a man for once in your life, and for you to lie like that. Shit was dead wrong." She is sitting there, crying with laughter while I am envisioning myself stabbing her.

"I am sorry, sis."

"Keep your sorry in a sac, asshole." I am so done

with her! Thankfully, we make it to the restaurant in the nick of time before I kick her out of my moving car.

WHEN WE ARE SEATED at SoleLuna Restaurant in Sunnyside Queens, we order two glasses of water and look over the menu. I order the burrata with heirloom tomatoes, which is creamy buffalo mozzarella with arugula and cherry tomatoes. Zamora orders the spaghetti alle cozze, which is spaghetti with mussels and a cherry tomato sauce. I have some of Zamora's dish, and it is amazing. We talk and get caught up with what is going on in our lives. Upon dropping her back to work, I urge her to think about dating.

Zamora has everything going for herself: a great job, an amazing home, great personality; you name it, she's got it. She had such a rough experience with men growing up, just one douchebag after another, but her last douchebag was close to 15 years ago. I've tried to set her up with many great men, but she always finds something detrimentally wrong, such as *He walks funny*, or *He's a Mama's boy*. I love her, but she needs to get it together.

CHAPTER THREE

It seems as if our romantic weekend never happened. Things have gone right back to normal between Naz and me.

I am starting to believe he is just not that into me anymore. I've tried many alternative ways for him to make love to me. If I could hang ass naked over my chandelier just so that he can fuck me, I would. I don't know how many thongs I have to wave in his face for him to touch me. Yes, I understand that after his boxing career came to an end, things haven't been the same. However, I can only come up with a few different scenarios to refresh our marriage. And nothing seems to be working.

I'm currently on school break, and all I want to do is lie beside him, watch old-time movies with a glass of wine, talk about absolutely nothing, and laugh. I just want my husband back.

"Nazzir, your phone is ringing in the other room."

I pass him, making my way into the kitchen from the workout room. We live in the Hamptons; he wanted a huge house due to his family size, and that's exactly what he got.

The house has bay windows that flow into the formal dining area with a skylight. Off the kitchen is a TV lounge with sliding glass doors leading to an oversized deck. There is also a guest bedroom and full bath on the same level. Upstairs, in a separate wing, you'll find the spacious master bedroom with a stylish bath and double vanity. Two additional bedrooms and a third bath. There's an attached two-car garage and a partially finished lower level with a home gym.

The outdoor has a relaxed deck overlooking the open backyard, which we purposely landscaped for privacy, where there is also plenty of space to play and enough room for an inground pool that we have yet to install, since we are minutes from local beaches. The house is just amazing. We decided to move out here several years ago from Queens, and I don't regret it! It's beautiful. Peaceful, quaint, and full of diversity. The only downfall is being damn near three hours from NYU, but it is so worth the travel…

"Good workout, baby?"

"I had an amazing workout, but now I must get out of these funky clothes. Do you care to join me in the shower?" I hold my breath, hoping he'll say *Hell fucking yeah,* but knowing him, he is going to say *No, baby, not tonight.*

"Yes, baby, I'll join you, I'm right behind you."

Wait, hold up, no, he didn't just say that! I am ecstatic; I actually skip to the bathroom.

I wait in the shower until I am freezing, with wrinkled fingers. Of course he never shows up. It is no surprise. I finally make it out of the bathroom, and there he is, sleeping like a bear. I'm surprised he doesn't have his thumb in his mouth. I stand there looking at him for damn near an hour without the slightest idea of what to do with our marriage. How many times can you go through the motions, how many times can one go through heartache, praying that things will eventually change, knowing deep down they won't? This man is all that I know. He was my first, and I thought that he was going to be my last. I decide to sleep in the guest room just to clear my mind.

CHAPTER FOUR

A t the end of the semester, I figure I'll quickly shoot to the bar to celebrate. I go to a spot near Chelsea Pier, which is about 10 minutes from NYU. Chelsea Pier is a historic area in the New York City borough of Manhattan. It's a designated historic location for tourists, amazing food, shopping, and nightlife; this spot is for sure the place to be.

"Excuse me, would you like another drink?" says the bartender.

"Yes, please, I'll have another round of the same. Thank you." I've been here for about an hour; I'll have one more drink, then I'll be on my way.

Looking around, I see that the spot is packed. The music is jamming, and people are really getting down on the dance floor. There is this one annoying-ass dude in the middle of the nightclub, that thinks he is Michael Jackson busting those funky dope moves. There's always an impersonator in every club!

"I hope you are having a good night; may I get you another round?"

I am going to pretend I did not hear this dude.

"What are you drinking tonight?"

I guess ignoring his ass didn't cut it! I roll my eyes with hopes they'll indicate that I want to be left the fuck alone... NOPE. Sadly, there is an open barstool next to me... Go figure!!

"Are you alone?"

Okay, by this time, I am done sizing up this dude. He is gawwwgeous... I mean, 6'3, dark-skinned, clean-cut, muscular built, and smells like heaven.

"I am married, sweetheart."

He gives me a puerile look. "I can see that you are," he says while pointing to my ring. So why in the world did he approach me?

"Okay... So what can I do for you?" I reply with a crooked grin. While waiting for his reply, some of his friends come over with just a little too much alcohol in their system.

"So you left yo boys for a beautiful lady, I see, iight, I am not knocking it, bro."

He glances over to me. "She is beautiful, isn't she?"

I yawn so loud, and his whole team starts laughing.

"You cold for real," he says as he waves over the bartender. "Carole, can you please get another round for my guys and…" He looks at me, waiting for me to answer.

"Just call me Z."

"…And a drink for my lady friend Z. By the way, my name is Mike."

Well, come to think of it, I guess one more drink won't hurt….

Two hours later, I am on the dance floor grinding hard on this dude; I mean R. Kelly *bump n grind* type swag! We're laughing and falling over each other. I cannot believe I got here, so drunk my stomach is starting to turn, wanting to vomit all over this perfect stranger.

He just doesn't let up. I am trying to stand my ground, seriously, but obviously, I'm failing miserably! Looking down at his watch, I realize it is slightly past 2 am. I freak out.

"Mike, I have to go, it is way too late, and my husband is probably losing his mind!" I know damn well he isn't… Nazzir is probably sleeping like a baby.

"Can we ditch this place for a second and walk the pier?" Our eyes meet. He starts pressing up against me, and as effortlessly as I can, I tell him to back away, but he knows from my weak expression that I am bullshitting. He grabs my hand and leads me outside to walk the pier.

"So they call you *Z*, huh?"

"Zadie is my name, Mike." Damn, his eyes are melting my insides!

"Why are you so bashful?"

"It is probably the liquor; and look around you, we are at one of the most romantic locations in NYC."

I haven't been to the pier for so long. The view of the Hudson River is astonishing. I can't remember the last time I was here; must have been over seven years ago.

"The view is amazing, but these yachts are just breathtaking. I would love to have a nice glass of wine, look up at the stars, and just chill on the deck of a yacht."

He stops and looks at me.

"Can I try something, Zadie?"

My eyes widen. "No, you cannot!" I give him the crazy eye look, thinking it would faze him, but it doesn't.

"Z, why are you out here with me then? Wouldn't you think if I wanted to do anything to you, I would've already?"

Yeah, he has a point… So I concede. He leads me through the outside crowd.

"What is it exactly that you would like to try?"

While walking down the pier, I am taken aback when he directs me onto a beautiful luxury yacht that has the initials *GM* on the side.

"This is yours?!" I ask as emphatically as I can.

"Ladies first." He points to the entryway. I walk my way onto the dock and into his yacht. Upon entering, it has a sense of glamour and luxury and textured fabrics that create a calm and comfortable ambiance. The color palette is harmonious, with unique combinations for each area, and the scheme flows throughout the entire yacht, from what I am able to see.

The yacht is functional and cozy, panoramic glass sheet windows, sensory lighting systems, and a built-in aquarium. It has a large drop-down television. I also notice on the next floor that there is a bar and a family room for entertainment. High-quality speakers operate throughout the entire yacht.

"Wow, this is breathtaking. What do you do for a living if you don't mind me asking?"

"I am an electrician." What a bold-face fucking lie! He is completely fabricating! I look at him and chuckle.

"Yeah… an electrician, huh?"

"Would you like a glass of wine?" he asks,

completely disregarding my sarcasm.

What the hell, I am living on the edge tonight!

"Yes, red, preferably."

Moments later, I feel him take a seat right beside me as he hands me the glass of wine.

"So what do you do for a living, Z?"

"At this time, I go to NYU School of Medicine."

"A doctor!?" he says with astonishment.

"Yes, well, soon to be."

"That is astounding!" Mike and I sit back and just chill, shooting the breeze for probably close to an hour. Before I know it, he's tracing his finger around my shapely lips and begins kissing me...

"No-no-no-what are you doing, who do you take me as!?" I break our kiss as I detach myself from his hold.

"Z, tell me you don't want this?"

He pulls out his fully erect man muscle.

"Sit on it," he instructs. I am completely taken aback and oddly turned on as my fluids speak for themselves.

"Fuck no, and fuck you, Mike," I spit as I open the yacht doors. He swiftly stands up behind me and slams the door. I am breathing heavily as he stands extremely close behind me; I can feel his toned chest and erect muscle. He wraps his arms around my waist and pulls me closer.

He whispers in my ear, "I'll ask again. Tell me you don't want this, Z…"

"This is wrong, Mike, completely wrong."

"But doesn't it feel right?"

He slowly unzips my dress while blowing on the nape of my neck. But I don't stop him. Who am I fooling? I want this just as bad as he does. As my dress floods the floor, I step out of it, and there I am, standing there in my black lacy sheer lingerie. He leads us back to the wing chair and begin to rub on his crotch. He frees his cock.

"Put me in your pussy."

I am in the mood to be outgoing, different, and feisty, so… I sit right on it! I don't know this man from a hole in a wall, but I am beside myself, and I don't care, not one bit.

I straddle him with one leg planted on the floor and the other leg over his shoulders. Mike sits there, moaning and relishing every moment. Then he lifts my other leg over his shoulders and begins to eat my pussy. I allow this man to indulge on my pussy for almost a half an hour. I lose how many times I come in his mouth.

"Put my dick in your ass," he whispers.

I have no idea what to say. I've never completed such a task before, but I don't care. I turn around, place his dick in my mouth, give it one nice deep-throat, then turn around so I am now straddling him. I slowly put him in my ass.

"Oh my God, Mike!" I scream so loud. It takes about 10 minutes before his fully erect penis completely enters my asshole. Quite frankly, it isn't very pleasurable in the beginning, but it feels amazing afterward. Eventually, I forgot his dick was even in my asshole.

He whips his dick out of my ass and tells me to suck it. I give him the craziest look. It is so outlandish, spontaneous, and different from what I'm used to; he is demanding, powerful, and vulgar, which turns me on even more.

As nasty as it is, I do it. I begin pleasuring the tip of his cock; I keep throwing it in the back of my mouth, allowing it to hit the back of my throat. I then form a pace that he can't resist. He keeps saying my name and grabbing my hair, his toes curled and legs extended.

I know he is desperate for release. Moments later, he is quivering. I stand there with his penis in my mouth, staring at him.

"Where have you been my whole life, Zadie?"

I immediately get up from the floor and begin to pace heavily across the room.

"I can't believe I just did that; I cannot believe I really just did that. I need to get out of here."

I am putting on my clothes one item at a time while still pacing. He tries to communicate with me, but I am zoned out, and I do not hear a word he is saying.

"What the fuck do you mean, you have to leave? Zadie, can you just relax, please?"

"Mike, I have to get home. I am married; I've never cheated on my husband! This isn't right."

"It feels right to me, though," he states as he stands over me.

"And what am I supposed to do with that, Mike? That doesn't mean anything to me. I just need to get the fuck out of here right now!"

He stands there, shaking his head in disbelief. I put on my platforms and run to the door. As I am exiting, he quickly runs over to me.

"I enjoyed my evening with you, Zadie. Sorry it had to end like this. Please don't be a stranger." He hands me his business card.

I open the door and run out; I am completely humiliated and embarrassed that I stooped this low.

Now I have to go home to my husband, who probably doesn't even know I'm missing in action. I galivant back to the bar; thankfully, it is still open. I ask the bartender for a glass of water. I run to the bathroom to get myself together, go to my car, and head home.

CHAPTER FIVE

A warm body is over me as my eyes open toward the sunrise.

"Baby, why did you sleep in the guest room? I was waiting for you last night." Who does he think he's lying to... I could have had a loud party, and he would not have budged, not even a little.

"I am sorry, baby, I came in here to gather some clothes, and then went to sleep."

"Okay, baby, well, I made breakfast. Sausage, eggs and cheese, French toast, a pumpkin pie with freshly squeezed orange juice."

Well, well, well.... impressive. Then again, I am not too surprised he knows his way around the kitchen, but to a certain degree, he wasn't a chef or anything. But some days, he damn sure gets down in the kitchen.

"Sounds delicious, baby. I'll be down in a minute."

"Please do. We don't want the food to get cold."

He kisses me on the forehead and makes his way back down to the kitchen. I run to the bathroom, wash my face, brush my teeth, look at myself in the mirror, tell myself, *It's going to be a great day,* and then make my way downstairs to have breakfast with my husband.

As I sit on the opposite side of my pub table, I am trying my best not to seem as if I am hung over and just giving myself away to any man.

"Are you okay baby? You don't seem like yourself."

I run to the kitchen sink so damn fast and let loose like I'm that chick in the exorcist movie. Vomit is everywhere. Nazzir runs over to me, pulls my hair away from my hair, and starts patting my back. I appreciate what he's doing, but I wonder if it's genuine. He barely ever touches me. Then again, maybe he is on this new leaf. I guess we'll just have to wait and see.

"Thank you; I'm not sure what came over me."

"Maybe a stomach bug. You must've had some something terrible to eat."

What! I can smell the alcohol damn near two miles away!

"Yes, baby. I'm sure it was the sushi I had for lunch."

"How about you go to bed and rest. I'll refrigerate

breakfast for another time. I'll make you some toast and tea to soothe your stomach."

"Naz, you went out of your way to make us this amazing breakfast. I'm not going to pass this up."

I am so adamant about eating his amazing breakfast, I walk back over to the table, sit down, take one look at the plate, and run back to the kitchen sink to vomit yet again.

I decide to take his advice and go upstairs to get some rest. He does exactly what he said he was going to do and makes me toast and tea.

Throughout the day, he caters to my every need. He keeps my medication and soup in rotation every four hours. He is definitely a godsend.

I've been in bed all day watching repeats on TV, and Naz has been lying next to me just about the entire day. I am completely impressed by his actions, yet it is also making me feel even more troubled by what occurred last night.

It is close to 8 pm, and I have been knocked out pretty much all day. Moments later, my doorbell rings, and I figure it's one of Nazzir's friends. But surprisingly, it's Shelly. Shelly has been a close friend of mine since the first semester of college, and we've been kicking it since.

Besides my sister and my husband, she's my go-to

person. Not sure what brought her to my home at this hour; I hope she's okay.

"Hey, chica!" she says as she makes her way up the stairs.

"I know it's extremely late. I've been hitting your phone all day to no avail, so I got worried and came to check on ya! But baby girl, what is your deal?" She looks at me in disgust.

"Well, thank you for clearly pointing out that I look like shit."

We laugh out loud.

"Don't get me wrong; you smell like shit too, baby."

I practically push her off my bed, I'm laughing so hard. Naz walks into the room.

"How are you able to deal with her looking this way?" Shelly states jokingly, and Naz stands there, staring at me.

"However she looks and smells, she is all mine."

He walks over and plants a soft kiss on my lips. I'm really starting to get this feeling that he knows I did something terribly foul last night. Or it may just be my guilty conscience. We have been on the edge of our marriage for quite some time, yet this is the most connection I've felt from him in a while. Sitting there pondering, I hear Shelly calling my name, but I'm unable to snap out of my thoughts. After she calls my name several times, Shelly stands in front of me and snaps her fingers to alert me.

"Girl, those meds got you tripping. Are you okay?"

Naz intervenes. "I'll start your bath if you're up for it."

"Of course, baby. Thank you. I'll be down shortly."

Shelly looks at me just as I was thinking, *Well, he's mighty charming.*

I hear the shower running. "Shelly, we need to talk like yesterday. Are you free tomorrow?"

"Yes, I am. Is everything okay, chica?" Her eyes are full of worry.

"Yes, I'm good. We just need to talk. I'll text you the time and location sometime tonight, okay?"

"Okay, chica, I'll be waiting."

I feel so much better than this morning, so I decide to walk Shelly to the door. I can't believe how terrible I felt today. I was lopsided, throwing up all over the damn place, not to mention that banging-ass headache I had.

Most people would say, *I am never drinking again* after an episode like this. However, this is the end of the semester, so I will more than likely drink again tomorrow.

"Baby, your bath is ready!" Naz yells from down the hall.

While walking toward the bathroom, I notice a raspberry scent coming from the same direction. I open the door, and there he is, sitting on the edge of the tub, candles lit, the tub filled with bubbles, and a glass of fresh ginger ready to soothe my stomach while I relax.

"Wow, baby, what do we have here?" I'm grinning from ear to ear. "This is so lovely, Naz, thank you." I lean in and kiss him.

"Do you mind if I get in with you?"

I look at this fool as if he has two heads. "Seriously, baby, you asked if I mind? Of course I don't mind!"

He removes my robe and nightdress while I remove his final piece of clothing. I step into the tub, and he follows. He sits with his legs around me, using the loofah to wash my back. He reaches for the remote to turn on the music.

We love our old jams, from Marvin Gay and Stephanie Mills to Barry White. So I know whatever satellite station is on, it's a good one.

"Feels good, baby?" he whispers in my ear.

I turn to him and say, "Yes, baby, it sure does."

"Z, I know things haven't been the same since—well, you know, since the accident."

The medications have been giving us a hard time with erections. I begged for him to stop taking the medications and seek an alternative option so that we can have a life again. However, he felt it was best to stay on that particular medication.

"I understand, baby, yet now is not the time to talk about it. Let's just enjoy this moment."

He starts touching my breast and teasing my nipples with his soft fingers while kissing my nape. Due to the night I had a few hours ago, since penetration is not an option, I am at ease.

He begins to play with my pussy under the water. He turns me around, grabs both legs, and places them over the side. At this time, the majority of my legs are completely out of the water and dangling over the tub. He gets out, kneels before me, opens my legs, pulls me closer to him, and pampers my pussy with his tongue. He drains the water just enough to be able to eat my pussy. I clamp my hands over his shoulders and begin to moan loudly; the lower half of my body begins to tremble as he moves faster and faster. He's eating my pussy as if he needs my juices to survive. Moments later, I come in his mouth. He dries my body, then carries me over to our bed, and we call it a night.

CHAPTER SIX

W e stare at each other for quite some time until Shelly breaks the awkward silence.

"What the hell, Zadie? Yeah, okay, you were drunk. However, that is never an excuse. I am extremely disappointed in you!"

During class, I whispered to Shelly to meet me at our normal hangout spot, the *Cafe Indulgence,* which isn't too far from Shelly's residence. Shelly lives in Freeport, NY, a village in the town of Hempstead, Nassau County, which is on the South Shore of Long Island, about an hour from NYC and slightly over two hours from my home.

Shit, she is absolutely right. I have never been the type to make up excuses. I was just so upset with Naz for dismissing me, and unfortunately, I lost it emotionally in the next man's arms.

"I am not blaming it on the alcohol, Shelly. He came on to me, and I liked it. Sadly, at that time, I wasn't in the correct state of mind. I will be honest with you; I loved the way he handled me. As gross as it may sound to you, he went straight to the point. Handled me like a man should. I can't stop thinking about him. Before I ran out of his yacht, he dropped his card on me; I haven't stopped looking at it. It was not the love and the affection I was looking for, which made it even more interesting. He was aggressive, and as I said before, he got straight to the point."

Shelly takes a sip of her tea. "So what now, Z? Are you going to continue seeing this guy?"

I am lost for words; I can't think of anything else to say. Yes, I should automatically say *Absolutely not, I will never see him again!* It is unfortunate that it took me several minutes to even come up with an answer.

"Shelly, I am not going to see this guy again. You know I love my husband more than life itself. After several years, I am finally beginning to feel good about our marriage. I never want to do anything to jeopardize what we have."

I think I just lied to my best friend! I can't believe I

did that. Yet she gives me a look as if she is not convinced.

"What, Shelly, why the odd expression?"

"I am just surprised that all of this happened. I can understand if you guys were having marital issues, and even then, just end the marriage, move on, and focus on yourself. Not fuck some stranger you met in the club. Anything could've happened to you, Zadie. It seems as if you want me to support that type of behavior, and I won't."

I tightly close my eyes and take a deep breath. "You are right, sis; I can't argue with you. It will not happen again." I just want this conversation to be done and over with. Silence falls between us.

"Anyway, Z, are you going to eat?" Shelly asks. Perfect, change of topic it is!

"Honestly, after a day like yesterday, I will just have tea."

"Mmm-hmm, I bet, God don't like ugly, Zadie," Shelly says, shaking her head.

"Shit, Shelly!" I spit. "It was one accidental night, just one fucking night; I can feel your judgments all around me. I am done with this conversation." I drop a 10-dollar bill on the table and head out.

"You see, that's your problem, you don't want to

deal with matters head-on," Shelly says, running behind me.

"I'll face my own demons. I don't need your lame-ass therapy session."

As I'm walking to my car, she jumps in front of me. "Okay, okay. My bad, Z. I am upset because he could've been a dangerous person, and I might not be having lunch with you today." There is a brief moment of silence.

"I am trying to compute this chain of events that transpired for you. That was one scary move. Just imagine what your sister would say." Both of my eyebrows raise because my sister would literally get the lighter fluid and light my pussy on fire!

"Look, I messed up. It was a mistake, and it will not happen again. I give you my word."

"Z, you will always be my girl. I will never look at you less than. I understand shit happens; just be smart next time."

We hug and part ways.

THE MOMENT I get into my car, I keep replaying the evening with Shelly. I take several deep breaths to calm my nerves. Not only by what she said but because I actually enjoyed my dangerous night with this perfect stranger.

It is so unfortunate how generic, or should I say mechanical, my husband has become. After some years, a woman needs some dick. I've suggested toys; he doesn't want to incorporate them. What else am I to do? I've suggested so many different things we could do, yet he turns down all of my proposals. I should be filled with so much pain and regret; however, oddly enough, I am not, not one bit.

Mike demanded my attention the whole night. Even though I was playing hard to get, he never gave up. His aggression was on point. He commanded my energy. As we danced through the night, his broad shoulders rippled through his shirt. His touch was firm, yet very passionate. We were immersed, as if it was just us two in the loud-ass club. He grabbed my mid-back and danced with me while our eyes locked. He held on to me very firmly, with so much tension. Throughout the whole night his energy sent signals up my spine.

Suddenly I am interrupted by a loud knock on my car window.

"Hey, baby, are you okay? Are you coming inside?" says Naz. I completely forgot I was just sitting in my driveway using my vibrator and having these thoughts.

"Of course, baby. I will be there in a few." Thankfully he does not stay to wait for me, since my mastur-bation session was just at its peak. As I watch Naz enter our home, I place my vibrator on max to quickly end this pleasurable moment. I think of what Mike and I shared that night, his smell, his aggression, and there I am at my full climax, legs shaking uncontrollably, short shallow breaths, with my eyes closed.

I take out his card and stare at it for nearly fifteen minutes. Yet I can't gather myself to call. Fuck it, let me get my ass in the house.

CHAPTER SEVEN

"Hey, girl, you better snap out of it." I hear an abrupt hand clap. Shelly is not only my classmate, but she is also my sister from another mother. If I am slacking for even 30 seconds, she is always there to pick me up. We have been riding with each other from day one of class. Many others left the program due to cost, difficulty learning, or lack of time. Yet Shelly and I have made it through.

Don't get me wrong; since this program is enhanced, many things are not the same, as years are shaved off. Trust me; there have been many days I thought of leaving this accelerated NYU School of Medicine Program. The path to becoming a doctor is quite sacrificial and can be a long road. My classmates and I have to embody a sense of selflessness in this pursuit. However, we are managing and making it through the best we can.

"Girl, what are you talking about? I am focused and wide awake," I state with a grin.

"Z, do you wish to talk during the break? I know that you're going through a lot…"

I'm not really sure what to say… I'm damn sure not going to tell her that I'd like to see Mike again so he can fuck my brains out…Or how I'm no longer into my husband because he has a shriveled dick and how it is changing the trajectory of our marriage.

How do I get out of this? I glance at the clock, knowing class is just about over. I take a sip of my coffee. "Why do you figure I need to talk?"

"Never mind, Zadie!" She walks out of the class and doesn't even bother to look back.

What can I say? I'll speak with her some other time, just not at this moment.

Several hours pass after Shelly stormed out of class, and since then I haven't received one text from her. I know she was in her feelings, so I decide to sneak into her apartment. Shelly is standing in the middle of her bedroom floor and gives me the most cynical look.

"Heyyy Sheeeelly." I'm playing this role as if everything is good between us.

"Yeah, okay, Z, excuse me, I need to get into my kitchen." She damn near pushes me down.

"What the fuck, Shelly!" I yell.

She stops in her tracks and heads back toward me. "You are acting very funny, Zadie. I don't know what the deal is with you, but I thought we were best friends. Yes, not as close as you and Zamora, but close enough. If we can't talk or trust each other, then what do we have?"

She walks out of the room and goes straight into the kitchen. I follow.

"We cool, girl, stop bugging out on me!" I wave my hand.

"Maybe you should give me my house keys and leave." No, this bitch…

"Are you seriously taking it there, Shelly? What the fuck for?" At this time, I am all the way upset.

"So let me get this straight. Because I got personal shit that I chose not to discuss with you, you wish to end our friendship? Fuck you, Shelly!" I begin walking away, but backpedal and approached her.

"You know what, Shelly? How the fuck did you make this about you? Yet you claim to worry about me! You just couldn't think of me for one damn minute, could you? That maybe, just maybe, I am going through a lot. Perhaps the anniversary of my parents' death is soon approaching! Possibly because my husband, who I love and pine for, cannot make love to me and hasn't made love to me in quite some time! That all my injured husband could do is stick his fingers in my pussy or eat it, but only when he feels like it! Or how about due to his overabundance of medications, he now has a limp dick that doesn't get hard, and he doesn't wish to use toys! Or how I have to masturbate in my car to avoid being heard by my husband. Or how I have to make sure he doesn't kill himself—better yet, how I enjoyed risking my life so that I can feel alive again! So that a perfect stranger can make me come, and I *enjoyed* every minute of it. I can finally fantasize about real sex, as opposed to watching pornographic films. Or how I enjoyed another man more than my own damn husband, and I can't stop thinking about him. Have you ever been so utterly embarrassed you chose not to share this personal information with anyone, not even your own best friend?"

I know I'm jumping off the handle and snarling at her, but damn I am so upset and determined to make her feel like shit. I did not want to tell her what was going on in my life because she doesn't have to know every single damn detail.

Shelly glances down in dismay. I know I've made her feel extremely uneasy, but that was my point.

"I am so sorry, Zadie," she whispers.

I quiz her reaction. Her eyes are watering as she begins to cry.

"You should be sorry." I show no remorse as I leave her keys and walk out.

I GET INTO MY CAR, turn the ignition, and peel off, but I don't get far. I immediately pull over into an empty parking lot staring at a large dumpster that some little kids are smoking pot behind. They run off rather quickly, but the way I rushed into the lot, they must have thought I was police. Shit, the way I am feeling right now, I would love to smoke a joint too!

I spend several minutes staring into thin air, but my mind is running a 10K marathon. I decide to call my sis, Zamora, to try and calm my thoughts, but her line just rings out.

"Hey sis, I miss you so much right now, I miss them too — a considerable amount. Just been going through levels of emotions these past few days. I really need to talk to you, okay? We should get together soon. I love you."

So many thoughts are flashing through my mind, and my emotions are all over the place. So I decide to get out of my car and go for a short walk.... I need time just to get away, even if it is for only a few moments. I sit on a bench about five minutes away from my car. The cool breeze feels amazing.

"Hey, hey, can you hold that bus for me, lady?" yells this kid running toward the bus; I didn't realize this was a bus stop. I stand up to signal the bus driver, and in the midst of jumping to my feet, I drop my purse. Every damn item falls out! I bent over to pick it all up.

"*I miss that position,*" he says.

Who the fuck...? I turn around so damn fast. My heart drops, but when I look at him, my pussy hits the floor...

"Mike!"

"Hello, Z. Let me help me you with that."

I am in utter shock as we both stare at each other while picking up my hair comb, lipstick, and tampons off the damn ground. I am so nervous right now. I am trembling where I stand.

"Well, you look surprised to see me."

Surprised!? I can't tell the difference between Niagara Falls and what the fuck is going on between my legs right now... *Okay, hold your composure, Zadie, get your shit together.*

He reaches over, cups my chin, and kisses me. I immediately back away. I stare at the ground as I try to hide my excitement. As much as I want to stand my ground, I can't. I grab his collar, pull him in close, and continue our kiss. He looks even better than he did weeks ago. His strong muscles outline his entire shirt, his pecs are bulging, his shoulder-length locks are twisted to perfection, and the scent of coconut fills my nose. Almond-shaped brown eyes, perfectly trimmed goatee, athletic build, pearly white teeth beneath his full-size kissable lips, there stands beauty. Damn, he is surely sexy!

"Wait a second!" Mike holds both arms up and backs away. No, this dude did NOT just ruin this moment!

"What happened?" I say with an intense gaze.

"Aren't you married, Z?" Mike states sarcastically. He's seriously sending a measure of guilt I've never felt before through my body... I can't believe he said that. While gazing at him, I feel sick to my stomach. Really sick, and before I know it, I lean over and eject matter from my stomach right onto his shoes. He doesn't even move. He immediately begins rubbing my back.

"Don't touch me!" I spit as I wipe my mouth with the back of my hand. Of course, I have no tissue in my pockets or purse. I finally get the courage to look into his eyes.

"Mike, I will pay to replace your footwear and get

your clothes dry-cleaned. I am so sorry that this happened, please forgive me. I am so sorry, but I have to go."

I immediately speed-walk down several blocks to where my car is parked. I can't believe that I succumbed to my feelings and entertained him with sweet kisses. I am completely embarrassed and clearly not in the correct state of mind. I have no clue what I was doing, but most importantly, what the fuck is he even doing here? How did he find me? Was he looking for me, or did he just bump into me, which I highly doubt?

My heart rate quickly accelerates as my passenger door rapidly spins open. I turn to my right. Mike is sitting next to me.

"What the fuck are you doing, Mike? Get out of my car. Why are you following me?"

"You stay running, Z," he says as he grabs my hand and kisses my knuckle while keeping eye contact the whole time. A part of me wants to scream bloody murder, but I enjoy feeling sexually alive again. I haven't felt this wanted in such a long time.

I raise my eyebrow, giving him the impression I'm not impressed with his moves. But the uncertainty in his response keeps me on the edge.

"Mike, I need to go home, clean myself up, and so

do you, and now you have vomit all over my car from your footwear."

"I actually took off my sneakers prior to entering your car." I lean over to see if that is true, and lo and behold, he definitely has on only socks in my car. I start to laugh.

His hands softly creep around my neck.

"You're driving me insane, you know that? I couldn't stop thinking about you since our last encounter. You ran away from me then, and I don't want you to run out on me now. May I ask, were you ever going to call me?"

A mix of emotions is raging inside of me.

"How did you find me, Mike?"

"You wouldn't believe me if I told you."

"Try me."

"Turn around and look outside your back window. You see that cemetery? I was leaving walking toward as you were getting out of your car. I followed you as you walked several blocks. I wanted to call out to you, yet I didn't want to startle you. I saw everything, even when the kid asked you to stop the bus. I was admiring your body the whole way, which provoked me to kiss you on sight, and I deeply apologize about that."

I can't stop staring at him. I am mesmerized and

completely nervous, so I promptly look away, biting my nails.

Moments later I break my silence...

"I'm so sorry for your loss. Who passed, if you don't mind me asking?"

"Someone very dear to me," he replies. It seems as if I've hit a nerve; I sense a different vibe from him.

I just blurt out, "Dinner this weekend?" Then I gave myself a mental kick after asking that question. I had to break the silence, as it was becoming very uncomfortable.

"Of course, I'd love to."

He meets my eyes and then reaches for the door handle.

"I will let you go, Zadie; I am sure you have a lot to do. Do you still have my card?"

"Actually, I lost it."

I am lying through my teeth, and for some apparent reason, I think he knows that I am too.

"You lost it, or you threw it away?"

"Does it matter, Mike?"

He opens his wallet, pulls out another business card, and hands it to me.

He clasps his hands together and inhales deeply.

"Please do me a favor, and do not lose it this time. I'll see you soon. Text me your number and I will text you the location and time as well as the date for us to meet. Drive safe, baby girl."

That was it…. The man I had an affair with was just sitting in my car, and now we are planning a dinner date; what did I get myself into?

CHAPTER EIGHT

While driving, I am struck by reality. The thought of going home to lie next to my husband is unsettling…

Then I come to remember one time when he was playing his Xbox with one hand and playing with my pussy with the other. That's when I knew our relationship was over. He assured me of that. I feel so guilty thinking this way, especially with what he has been through….

My phone chimes with an incoming text from Naz.

Baby, please get milk. We are low, and you know I need my cereal. Love you, see you in a few, I hope.

- end of message would you like to reply-

Hey Honey. I am pulling up right now. Don't worry; I already bought milk. I love you too.

And there's my husband smiling upon my arrival while standing at the front entrance watering the lawn…I used to get so excited seeing him waiting for me. Well, I feel slightly excited, but not like I used to. It isn't like I don't love him; I just feel he is effortless when it comes down to pleasing me.

I get out of my car and sashay playfully to my husband down the walkway into our home.

"How was your day, baby?" he asks.

"You don't want to know," I say with a cynical laugh.

"Baby, how about we get away this weekend, someplace far, very discreet, and might I add romantic?"

"Away!! Oh my God, yes, of course." I lean in and kiss Naz. I purr, "Baby, you don't need to ask, ever. Just tell me when and I'll pack my clothes." Going away seems to be the only option that he has left to make me feel good. It does work, but I'd rather make love on these trips. I definitely don't want to seem like the ungrateful wife, but sometimes I do feel discouraged.

IT IS NOW 1 in the morning, and I can't shut off my mind. I have been lying in bed trying very hard to sleep; however, nothing is working. I am wide awake. The last 24 hours have been a whirlwind. So I decide to go into the next room to study. Two hours go by rather quickly. I am barely able to keep my eyes open. As I get back into bed, I check the news for headlines. Suddenly, before turning my phone off, I receive an incoming text from Shelly.

Hey, chica. I know it's crazy early in the morning, but you know me. I'm off to work in the wee hours, and knowing you, your phone is powered off anyway. Just know that I am extremely sorry for being selfish. I wasn't feeling well; it was my stomach. Must have been something in my pasta primavera that obstructed my normal way of thinking Lolz... I love you, chica. Moving forward, I will make sure I'm not only thinking of myself. Maybe one day after class this week, we can grab a coffee if you don't mind. Love you, goodnight or....

I wasn't able to read to rest of Shelly's text message; I was out cold.

"HOLY SHIT, baby, you have to wake up, we are so late!" I said while I was frantically waking up Naz and trying to hop in the shower. We have an appointment this morning with a real estate firm he is attempting to buy. He recently completed his real estate course and is now trying to build a brand; he is also a part of the NAR, the National Association of Realtors.

"Baby?" he says, stopping me in my tracks. "We are just about an hour late for the meeting; I've been up for a few hours already. I called and told them we need to postpone. It is currently rescheduled for next week. It is perfectly fine. You were up studying all night, and I knew you were not going to be able to make it, so I figured why not just go ahead and reschedule."

"Well, well, then, honey... I guess you took care of everything." I turn around and get back into bed, and he climbs into bed as well. In doing so, he crawls under the sheets, tosses my legs over his shoulders, and begins kissing my inner thighs, then slowly making his way up to tease my clit.

I then grab the back of his head, bringing his face deeper into my pussy. This time his pleasure feels different. He feels like the man that was determined to make me feel great. I moan and cry at the same time.

Mentally I have a lot going on, but physically at this moment, I want to endure every second while admiring the strikingly picturesque view of the sun rising. He stiffens his tongue, which is fixated on my enlarged clit. I begin to vigorously rub his head as I keep raising my ass off the bed, bringing the lower portion of my body closer to his mouth. I can't contain myself just lying there...Both hands now flat on the bed, I begin to gyrate harder. Naz is doing things that he hasn't done in such a long time. His craft is becoming better and better. His tongue stiffens and keeps ramming inside of my pussy as he moves his head quickly left and right while humming, with his fingers in my ass.

"Damn baby, what are you doing to me?" I place my head back down, up, then down again, while biting my bottom lip and closing my eyes. I practically try to run from him, but he has a massive hold of my legs... I couldn't get away even if I wanted to...

"Fffuckkk!" I begin to breathe uncontrollably; my legs begin to shake. "OH, SHIT SHITSHITSHIT Naz!" I scream over and over again; my thighs are getting so tight, and he is still slurping on my clit. My body goes into a vigorous spasm, clawing the sheets that lie beneath me. I think I've squirted a few times, but I've lost track. Naz and I make eye contact as he begins to blow on my clit, I guess to cool me down, not knowing it is doing quite the opposite.

"I love you, baby."

My brain is working in so many motions. *Is my husband back? Does he know I fucked Mike? Does he know Mike came to visit me? Did he catch me masturbating while looking at Mike's business card? Did Shelly call him?* So many thoughts are turning my mind.

Regardless, there is one thing that will never waver. The love for my husband.

"I love you too, honey." He kisses my inner thighs and moves his way slowly up to my navel. Lying vertically on my stomach, he inhales deeply as he holds my hand and says, "Baby, how long has it been?"

A ghost of a smile crosses my face. "How long has what been?"

"Since you've been seeing someone…"

I sit up on the bed, let go of his hands, and stare at him, practically shaking. "What do you mean, baby?" I can no longer look him in the eyes.

"Look at me, Zadie. How long have you been seeing someone else?"

"Are you out of your fucking mind? How dare you ask me that question, Nazzir!?"

Tears are rolling down his face.

"Baby, I am not seeing anyone. You know I would never hurt you."

I am utterly confused. How does he know? I never called, texted, or emailed Mike...

He stands up and starts shaking his head.

"You have been so distant with me, Z. I know you very well. We have been dating and married for a very long time. We grew up with each other. I may know you better than you know yourself. Yeah, iight I feel off, I get that. But don't go around fucking on me like you some type of nasty thot. I didn't mold you that way, and your parents damn sure did not raise you that way..."

I walk up to my husband, standing in front of him with my eyes clamped shut. I tightly hug him, and we are intertwined for several minutes. I then drop into a bawling fit at his feet. But he immediately lifts me up. He gasps, and I stare him in the eyes, uncontrollably crying, without saying a word. I am speechless. I can't lie to him anymore. He doesn't deserve this treatment. He looks back at me...

"Stop! Just stop seeing him before shit gets out of hand, do you hear me?" I nod my head. He kisses me on the forehead.

"Let's go shower." He cradles me like a child, bringing me into the bathroom while I am still crying with shame. We shower, and he lathers my hair and my body. Then he sits on the bench in the shower, turns me around, traces his finger over my navel, then starts softly kissing my waistline from left to right. He lifts his head and looks into my eyes.

"Zadie."

"Yes, baby?"

"I don't know what I will do if you leave me."

"Leave you? I am not going anywhere, baby. Don't talk like that." I grab his ears, then kiss him. He raises my left leg over his shoulder and begins to eat my pussy again. The nice warm water running on my back feels so good...

Since this is an en suite freestanding tub, I have nothing to hold on to but his head. I can't compose myself; my arms are moving everywhere, trying to control my urge not to spew my juices in his mouth.

"You taste so good. Release for me, baby," he whispers.

"I love you so much, Naz, I love you so much!" I scream as I release in his mouth again. Breathing rapidly, I brace my forehead on the shower tiles, placing my shaking leg onto the shower floor.

I start to cry again.

"Talk to me, baby."

"I don't know what I was thinking, Naz; I am so sorry. I just—"

Naz abruptly cuts me off. "We don't need to talk about it, ever. We'll fix our marriage. I know we will."

"Yes, we will."

CHAPTER NINE

"So, we cool?" asks Shelly.

"You know we are, don't sweat it. I clearly understand your points, and I hope you understand mine. Going forward, I will definitely make sure I am more honest and open with you to the best of my ability. Understand that everything doesn't need to be spoken out; if I am slightly distant and I don't tell you it's about you, then don't worry about it."

"Yes, chica, I'll appreciate that so much. Thank you."

"Girl, don't thank me. We will always be cool. Just don't threaten me again, that wasn't cool. Not even in the slightest."

"Hey, ladies!" I invited my sister. I haven't seen her

a few weeks. We would usually meet for lunch and catch up weekly; however, these last few weeks she has been pretty busy.

I get up and give her a bear hug. "I miss you, sis. What's going on? I'm starting to feel as if you are neglecting me."

"Oh, stop it, little sister. I will never neglect you. You're my other half; I've just been busy with work."

She seems to be acting brand new. Just the fact that she is smiling this hard is definitely not up her alley.

"Okay sis, so let's chat. How's work and the girls coming along?"

Zamora is in the process of buying her own studio for the girls. I am overly proud of her!

"Talk to me, sis, how is the studio hunting coming along?" I await her response, which takes nearly several minutes.

"It is going good…"

"Shelly, why does it feel as if I am talking to myself because my sister seems to be completely engulfed in her phone and not paying much attention to me?"

"Chica, it definitely seems as if she is not listening to you."

Shelly and I are having an indirect conversation while waiting for Zamora's attention.

"Ladies, ladies, please, I'm just texting my new guy."

I stare at her with my nostrils flared, eyebrows shrugged, arms crossed, just pissed the fuck off!

"Zadie, baby. I know that look. Relax, okay? We only started talking two days ago. I was going to tell you over the phone when we scheduled this lunch yesterday, but I wanted to surprise you."

I pray internally for a few seconds because I really thought I was going to snap. *Okay, okay, breathe, Zadie. Two days is not so bad.*

"You know me too well… I'll let this one slide since it was only two days. So spill the beans. What's his name, what does he do for a living, do you have any pictures, where did you guys meet? Omg, sis, I'm so ecstatic right now!!"

I believe half of the restaurant heard me. I am overly excited; my sister has been single for so long. She's such a beautiful person in and out, yet at the same time, she is such a very picky person. She has been through so much with men in her past that it's hard to trust them. I understand she is scared; we have all been there, but sometimes you just have to bite the bullet and let God lead the way.

Sis takes a sip of her wine. "Funny story, I went to get my car inspected, and we were both waiting for our number to be called. While I was reading, he asked the name of the book. Then we talked, and I learned he is a big reader, and obviously, you know I am as well. So we discussed books, authors, movie-related books, and before I knew it, as I was about to pull out of the parking lot, he knocked on my car window and asked for my contact information. When he reached home, he texted me a picture of his massive bookcase and provided a list of books he suggested I read. His name is *Oscar*. He's an engineer like your husband, but I believe he is what you call an industrial engineer; he designs control systems or something like that, I'm not quite sure yet. We really didn't dig deep into our careers because we were so involved with talking about books, but trust me, I will definitely get back on that topic. I tell you, ladies, he is so handsome and even more attractive because he is into books. If you know me, you know I love my books, so I will have to say thus far I am pretty impressed, but again it's only been two days. So to answer your question, that's who I've been texting: Oscar."

"Sis, you were smiling so hard while telling us that story! I love it! However, you know he has to pass the *sisterly interrogation protocol,*" we all say in unison, laughing so loud. They know the drill, and I am not playing! When my sister meets a guy, I am there full front and center.

No man is allowed to cross any threshold without my interrogation, and she does the same. Granted, she is older, and I haven't been on the dating scene a lot prior to Naz, but even the handful of men that I've dated, she was always on point, and I did the same with her.

We will arrange a meeting; usually, all three parties will go out for coffee, and I will then interrogate the guy. After I complete the grill, if for any reason I disapprove, she will dig a little deeper into him then cut him loose if need be. We are that amazingly close.

"Well, sis, I will give you a few more days with this guy before we set up our meet and greet; how does that sound?"

"Sounds good to me."

"Can't wait to meet him!"

"Yes, I think you'll like him. He is a straight-up kind of guy, hardworking, very smart, and girls, he is tall, dark, and yummilicious!"

"Yummilicious, sis?" I'm laughing so hard. "That is a new one. I can't decide if that was pretty good or very lame!"

"I think it was pretty lame," Shelly says.

"Shut up, the both of you!" Zamora says as she nudges Shelly, both laughing.

"Lame it is," I retort.

"Needless to say, Zamora, I am very happy for you, and if I am thrilled, I can only imagine how your sister is feeling internally right now."

"Fireworks are exploding in me right now, ladies," I say with so much excitement. I then grab Zamora's hand. "All jokes aside, sis, you deserve to be happy. The right man will love you unconditionally. After a long and hard road with men, I know it hasn't been easy. I can't say that I know what you are going through because I haven't been hurt, but you are my best friend, and I feel your pain. Even when we have a major falling out, we always regroup. We are only apart for such a small percentage of the time, and even then, I can still feel you. Every time you went through something, I was there internally as well as physically. I felt everything you were going through with each and every guy that hurt your feelings and abused you. Hey, and if this one doesn't work, you'll keep fighting, right?"

Zamora nods.

At this time, we are all quiet. She has damn sure had her share of dirtbags, men who abused her physically as well as mentally, called her job, got her fired, stalked her, killed her dog—and that is only the half.

God, I remember I had to tussle with this one guy to get off of my sister because she didn't want to eat pork! I just couldn't believe how much of jerks those men really were.

"Well, this was nice, ladies. We should really do this again, and not once every six months!" Shelly states.

She is absolutely right. As a group with my two favorite girls, doing this two times a year doesn't cut it...

"How about all of us agree on the date right now and put the reminder in our phones?" We all agree on the next date, which is in two weeks. We promise we will make sure this happens as faithfully as we say it should. We pay the bill and walk to the front. We depart from Shelly, but sis and I stay back for a few minutes.

"Heading home or to the library?" Zamora asks.

"I am not sure yet. Things been going good with Naz and me, so I think I'll go home to my husband tonight, lay low, and watch some movies. I'll just catch up with assignments tomorrow. What are your plans, seeing your boo thang? Oh no, correction, your yummi-licious?" Laughter bursts out between us two.

"No. I have a few recitals coming up, probably go to the studio and square off a few things. We plan on meeting for dinner this weekend."

"This weekend, as in two more days?"

"That is correct, sis."

"But I didn't meet him yet; this is going way too quick. This isn't what we do. Why are you changing?"

"Don't be upset, but I think I am getting too old for—"

I eye her warily and cut this woman right off mid-sentence. "Don't you dare say that, Zamora. I am going to pretend I did not hear the start of that sentence; I am stunned that you even said that. How could you say something like that?"

She angles her body toward me. "As I was saying… I think I am getting too old for the waiting game. Not your *sisterly interrogation protocol.* If only you just allowed me to finish my sentence. Of course I want you to meet him. I am just anxious to see what he is about. It has been a while, a very long time that I even felt the closeness of a man, took a whiff of a man's cologne. Damn, not to mention sex! Not saying I am going to jump into bed with Oscar tomorrow, but I really need intimacy and not just sex."

"Oh, I know, all right. You had me scared for a moment, but I completely understand, I do. I am sorry I overacted."

"You are perfectly fine. I don't blame you. This

interrogation process is a must. But enough about me, what is going on with you?"

Talking about me is a not a good idea. I tell my sister everything, but she will disown me for a long time if I tell her about my affair. I have to do what I always do and move the conversation back, always a good ploy... One day I will tell her everything, just not right now.

"Zamora, are you gaining weight?"

"What? NO, I am not! Girl, I look fat?" She presses down on her stomach, swaying her body left to right. And just like that, we were off the topic.

"Nah, I am only playing, sis. You look beautiful as always."

"Girl, don't scare me like that. Now is not the time, especially since I am about to go on my first date in ages."

"Oh, oh, why the worry expression? What is wrong? Zamora, talk to me."

"Why do you think something is wrong with me?"

"Because I know you very well, and you have that worrisome expression on your face."

"Well, I guess I am just nervous. When I said I haven't been on a date in so long it literally hit me. It's been years since I have allowed myself to open up to someone other than you. I just don't want this to go wrong as all the others. I meet the worst men. They all seem to be overly aggressive and intimidating. It doesn't matter where I meet them; they all end up the same."

I don't know what else to say after her vent. I know it's hard to get back on the dating scene, especially after all she has been through; I don't know how many times I have to tell her she's an amazing person that meets the wrong type of men.

"You know none of that is your fault, right? None of their actions were because of anything you did. They were possessive and overly jealous. You are beautiful, successful, you live on your own, no kids, educated, and you're funny. You are a great catch, sis, and now you are about to own a dance studio. Girl, you are doing it, and if a man doesn't appreciate the woman you are with all of your achievements and endeavors, then he doesn't deserve you. Right now, this guy seems to be on your level or may even be above your level, and that is someone you need. If they are levels beneath you, they will feel intimidated, and looking back, that was the case. Even when you were younger, you had so much going for yourself, whether it was attending one of the most prestigious dance schools, having ambition, or even yours and mine relationship. A lot of men didn't understand that; it was overwhelming for them, and they ran off. That was years ago, sis. Just know things are different today. Men are not the same, some are worse, but there are many out there who are great."

"I know, we have been talking about this for so long. I am ready for change. I have confidence in myself that things will go right with whomever I date moving forward."

"I love you, sis. You got this, sis; I have faith in you."

CHAPTER TEN

I sit alone in the bar drinking a glass of red wine just to kill time. It has been several weeks since I confessed my affair to my husband. Since then, he's been surprisingly different. Actually, I won't say completely different; I'll say he's back to the person I fell in love with. However, he has been extremely stifling.

He is constantly calling, asking tons of questions. I'm sure he installed a GPS on my phone because there were times I bumped into him at random places, such as supermarkets, restaurants, even my school library....

"Is anyone sitting here? Would you mind if I take this stool?" I am startled and quickly turn around.

"No, not at all, please sit down. You really scared

me." I am unable to take my eyes off this stunning man sitting next to me.

"I noticed you the moment I walked in." Mike leans in close to me.

"Did you, and what did you notice?"

His face cools down, looking at me dreamily as he sucks on his bottom lip.

"Your scent. Can you order two of what she's drinking, Carole?" he says to the bartender. "So what are you doing on my side of town? You missed our date a few weeks ago. I waited two hours for you." He eyes me from head to toe like he wants to eat me up. Okay, so I forgot to mention... I am having a sip of wine at the same bar where I met Mike several months ago.

I start giggling; the shyness just can't stay away.

"What is funny, Z?"

"Mike, you do something to me that I just can't figure out. You unknowingly, innocently, or carefully intimidate me. You make me feel wanted, ashamed, sexy, and skittish at the same time, yet you soothe me. I know I shouldn't feel anything for you, but I do."

Mike gets up from the barstool and stands over me; he strokes my shoulder-length hair, then places a lock behind my earlobe. *He smells so good.*

"Let's go for a walk."

"As much as I would love to, Mike, I really don't want to go to the yacht nor walking with you."

"Who said we were going to my yacht? Let's just go for a walk, start over, talk about the normal things that we didn't get to do before."

"Maybe we shouldn't. That is way too personal, and I am married."

"Not happily. If you were, you wouldn't have been here to begin with, correct?"

He is right; I feel foolish for ever getting the balls to come here... I should not have opened this door. But even if I did, I should have closed it a long time ago.

My heart is racing and my eyes cloudy with tears. "Mike, I am sorry, but I have to go." I drop 40 bucks on the bar and run out.

"Zadie, STOP, please ..."

He runs after me; we are now in front of the club. He grips me from behind, grabs my hand, turns me around, pulls me in close, and begins kissing me aggressively. And I go right along with it. We are two maniacs outside of the club going at it like it is the end of days. After several minutes, we slow down, both breathing heavily, eyes closed, forehead to forehead contact.

"Mike, NO, I can't, I just can't do this!"

As reluctant as I am... I push myself away from him.

"Zadie, don't do this. Look at what you do to me; you feel this, you don't want me?" He places my hand on his fully erect penis. I can feel my pussy juice between my ass crack.

"*Naz*, I can't...... oh my, I meant, Mike. I am so sorry, I didn't mean to call you my husband's name." We stand quietly, just staring at each other.

"Zadie, you are right. I can't keep doing this with you. You're a married woman with probably loads of baggage. I don't know what I was thinking. I'm clearly the fool by believing you wanted me as much as I wanted you. I can't believe I expected more from a married woman. Good luck, Zadie, with school and the whole bit." He kisses my forehead, then turns and walks back into the bar.

I make it to my car, which is directly across the street. The moment I sit in my car, I fall into an emotional mess. Slamming my hands on the steering wheel, I say, "*Damn it, damn it, damn it!*" I can't remember the last time I've cried this much. *What mess did I get myself into?* In the midst of my emotional breakdown, I look toward the entrance of the bar, and there he is, just sexy as sexy can be, standing there with a distressed expression, watching me as I have my breakdown.

For several minutes we gaze into each other's eyes. I wipe away my tears, as well as all of my fears and guilts. I open the car door without breaking the stare. I climb into my backseat but leave the door open, hinting for him to come across. He doesn't come over immediately, so I assume he is having a conflict of his own... But moments later, he finds his way across the street into my car, then closes the door behind him.

"I hate seeing you this way," he says as he wipes the tears from my eyes.

"Don't talk."

I hungrily start to remove his clothes; he reciprocates my feelings, forcefully taking my clothes off as well. I place a condom on his dick and wrap my legs around his waist, fucking him like I missed him. He salivates on my face from chin to forehead, grabs my ponytail, and yanks my head back; I am staring at the top of the car while he is pinching my nipple softly with his teeth.

"Fuck this dick, Zadie."

I position myself on my feet to feel his dick deeper inside me. I go faster, harder, faster; our kisses became more profound as he keeps ramming his dick deeper and deeper inside of me. He cups my legs, which are now lying on his forearm as he begins to control my movement.

"Fuck!" He moans, then goes faster.

"Yes, yes, yes!" I scream. It feels so good, so deep, so rugged.

His hands slide under my thighs, gripping my ass cheeks from under me. My legs and calves are now swinging in the air; he has total control, ramming my body on his dick.

"Fuck, Mike!" I delete everything that is a bother to me and only think of what is going on between my legs.

As much as I do not want to come, I can't keep it in any longer. My pussy is soaking wet; this immense feeling in my body has taken over. I haven't been fucked like this in years. I just can't take it anymore; all I have in me is my orgasm to let loose.

"I didn't tell you to do that," Mike grunts. He lays me down with my neck curved on the door, his hands curled in at my waist, lifting my bottom half to his face as he begins drinking on my pussy.

"Ahhhhh!" This fucking motherfucker is devouring me!

"Jesus, Mike!" I groan and angle up as much as I can. He is a beastly, hungry, eating machine, firmly sucking on my aroused clit. I press down on my hands, pulling myself up toward his face and taking it all in. It feels so good. He places me down, takes off the condom, and comes over me, dick in my face.

"Put this dick in your mouth."

I eagerly do just that. His arm is braced on the back of the passenger seat headrest. I am now deep-throating his dick, but he is surely helping with that. He is ramming his dick in my mouth; I have absolutely gagged a few times.

"I like the taste of you," he whispers and goes right back to eating my pussy. Dear God. He's a savage!

"You can come for me now," he says very softly, and I do just that for the third time; I think I am light-headed, delirious, and seeing three heads. What is he doing to me?

Dear God, he is not done. I watch him put on another condom, and I'm ready for whatever he's got. He flips me over now and is fucking me from behind. Our bodies are close, and my legs are on the console in between the driver and the passenger seat, desperately trying to steady myself as he goes wild in me. He slams into me with force, pushing me into the car door.

"Fuck! You drive me insane!" he screams, one stroke at a time. Then he relaxes on my back. "Kiss me," he demands.

I turn my head around as much as I can; he grabs my chin and begins slipping his tongue into my mouth.

He slips out of me, turns me around in his arms, and cradles me.

"You look tired."

With a cloudy haze look in my eyes, I laugh under my breath. "I am very tired, but it was well worth it. I am sure my body will regret this tomorrow. We can only do so much in the backseat of a car, but we made it work. But Mike, I thought you wanted to talk…"

Still dropping kisses on me, he says, "If you would like, we can talk now."

"I'd like that, but I wonder what time it is."

"Let me check that for you." He begins looking for his phone in his pants as I start getting myself together.

"3:42."

"Holy shit, Mike! This is terrible. I should've been home! Gosh, I'm so fucking silly!"

I am hurriedly putting on my clothes.

"Baby, you have to relax. A few additional minutes will not make a huge difference."

"You don't understand. Things have been different with us, and I don't want things to turn bad again."

I rabidly grab Lysol wipes from the compartment, wipe the back seat down, then complete a visual search for any evidence.

Mike grabs my hand. "Baby, you are shaking and

falling apart. Come here." He moves my stray hairs behind my ear, then stares at me.

He rubs my hand with care. "You are gorgeous, Zadie. Please don't kill this moment, Z, not like this. I don't want to lose you, but I am willing to walk away just to avoid this look on your face."

"No," I say with shame, yet confidence at the same time. I exhale and place my head on his chest while he massages my hair.

"Maybe this is meant to happen, Zadie. I don't care how you rationalize why we shouldn't be together; it won't change how much I am into you."

"I am sorry, Mike. My mind is racing; I never imaged having an affair or lying to my husband. It is terrible how eager I am to see you; it has only been three months and our third encounter. Yet I haven't stopped thinking about you. I never expected things to turn out the way they did."

"I haven't been able to stop thinking of you either."

"But nothing good will come out of this, Mike."

"Maybe you are right, but how about we just see where this goes?"

I nod yes. He kisses the back of my hand.

"I should really get going, though."

We get fully dressed.

"I just have to ask. If you were single, would you be mine?"

There is nothing more of a turn-on than a man who clearly wants me completely. The hunger in his eye gives off a power-driven shock between us.

"I don't know. We haven't had a conversation yet. At this point, we are driven off of sex, the hunger for each other, and loneliness." I touch his dick through his pants. "Your dick is still hard, which is great, but the sex is clouding our judgment and taking over our logical way of thinking. You should understand my point."

"Enough said, Z. I understand. We will definitely get to know each other a lot better, and we'll just cut out the sex," he says and gets right out of the car.

I follow. "Whoa, wait, what… I didn't say all of that!"

He stands there. This tension is overwhelming, my heart is racing, and my breathing pattern deepens. I lean against him on the car.

"Are you serious about cutting off the sex?" He is so handsome; I just can't help but to stare.

"Dead serious." His gaze locks with mine; he is not playing at all. His message is clear.

"Well, you are arrogant."

"Self-assured, not arrogant. I want you, Zadie, just

you. Go home, get yourself together; we will see each other again."

His eyes sparkle. I am beginning to long for him. I close my eyes, exhale, then re-open them.

"When?"

"Very soon. Have a good night, Zadie, and drive safe."

I wave bye, get into my car, and watch his sexy ass walk away.

CHAPTER ELEVEN

I've immersed myself in schoolwork—or at least tried to. I am here, but I am always deep in thought. Thinking about all the wrong I've done, thinking why Mike hasn't reached out to me in eight days. Thinking maybe our last encounter wasn't as special as I thought. Then again, it was in the backseat of a car... I have been so engulfed in thought and school that my husband has been questioning me a lot more than usual. Naz is the type that doesn't do well with inattention. Yet it is obviously clear that he became insecure after my confession.

Phone chimes--

Meet me at the Loveaday restaurant 2 days from now when the sun sets. Don't bother driving, take an uber, no need to respond unless you are unable to attend.

My body quivers, and I bite my bottom lip, smiling from ear to ear.

"Well, glad to see that someone is finally smiling; you've been so wrapped up in schoolwork. I haven't seen you smile in days; who was that on the phone, baby?"

Naz has entered my study at the wrong damn time!

"Hey, baby, ah, you know my sister is full of surprises. As you are aware, she is talking to this new guy, Oscar, and I'm so happy that she is finally dating! She texted a pic of them horseback riding, and I couldn't help but to smile."

"Again, I thought they just went horseback riding several weeks ago…" Shit! He's right.

"Silly me." I take a look at my phone and immediately delete Mike's text. "They actually went to play miniature golf."

He stares at me for a moment longer. Was my lie completely evident? This man knows me better than myself most times. I never played coy games with my husband before, but over the last few weeks, I've become a pro at it. He stands there, stroking his beard. A slow smile grips the corners of Nazzir's mouth.

"Baby, you are working too hard. When was the last time you even took a pause?" Naz walks to my work-station and sits on the edge of the table. I lower my lashes.

"Maybe several days." My focus is solely on Naz; I stare at him for several moments.

"You seem distant, preoccupied. How about we go dancing this weekend? Tell your sister and she can bring this new guy of hers." He caresses my cheek. "What say you?"

"Of course, baby, that sounds like a great idea!"

My eyes widen with excitement. I jump up from my seat and cradle myself in his arms.

"I can't wait to go dancing; it's been a long time. How about Saturday?" Two days from today will be Friday, and I already have plans.

"Saturday works fine with me, baby; your happiness is all that matters." He squeezes me tightly and brushes his mouth over my temple, then cups my chin and kisses me.

"Zadie." Naz's soft tone melts me all the time.

"Your happiness is all that matters to me. Wrap things up, and let's go to bed."

I nod without hesitation. "I'll be there in a few."

THE NEXT TWO DAYS, I am full of anxiety, wondering what to wear for both events. I want to look edgy, sexy, and classy, all at the same time. I am giddy and excited, especially since my sister is more than willing to come dancing with us.

"Hey, sis! Are we going to the mall today? We have to get ready for this weekend. I can meet you there after my a.m. classes; how does that sound?"

"Yes, yes, and yes!! let's do this! Which mall?"

"How about the one near my school? Come to think of it, you can pick me up as opposed to taking two cars."

"Okay, sounds good. However, one o'clock will not work. Are you able to wait until two o'clock? I have a meeting with the dance group."

"Yes, that is just fine; I will go into the study hall and work on some assignments. See you then."

This is the best part of my week, doing something out of the normal. Going to the mall, chilling out with my sister, sipping on Surf Squeeze, eating Nathan franks, and Tutti Frutti yogurts as if we were back in high school.

We will typically go to Barney's and have clothes tailored, but this seems to be a casual, spur-of-the-moment kind of event, and we can still look dashing shopping at Bloomingdale's and Nordstrom.

"Zadie, it is terrible to eat first then go shopping. You know I get tired."

We laugh.

"It's best to eat, then work it off while shopping!"

"I suppose."

"So what's going on, Zamora? How are things with you and Oscar?"

Her smile is extreme, her eyes wide with excitement as she takes a spoonful of her frozen yogurt.

"He's my kind of guy, sis. He's charming, educated, family-oriented, a hard worker, and simply amazing. I've been single for quite some time because I need someone to understand the passion of working and building, which he does. I do not have to sacrifice work because he requires all of my time. You met him, so you know he is extremely funny and down to earth. Bottom line, he is a great person to be around all the time. There is no Hallmark card that can capture this man... Oh my goodness, sis! I didn't tell you!!! I am going to be on the *nonstop* show next month! Oscar gave me the connection, and I went for it! This is a great opportunity for me, Zadie. I can finally grab the attention to reach a wide targeted audience. Consumers feel more comfortable with brands that are advertised on the media. This new branding is large for me. I finally have the opportunity to utilize several avenues to display my talent and my girls'! It will send a message that I am a reputable and well-established dance company."

"Are you kidding me? This is astonishing news, sis!!" I quickly get up and give her a tight, long hug.

"You know I do volunteer work for them! That's a huge company. You struck gold, sis! Your luck is finally falling in place, a new guy, and great new opportunities. They say success usually comes to those who are too busy to be looking for it, and this is a prime example. You were so wrapped up in work, and you kept pushing people away because of work. Now here you are, you may have finally found true happiness and not only with Oscar, but your life. We are no longer having those same old discussions about you needing a man to provide some fun in your life..."

Zamora jokingly waves me off. "Whatever."

"I love you, sis."

"I love you most, lil sis. Now let's go shopping!"

We place our remains in the trash bin and start to head south of the mall toward Bloomingdales. The mall is packed, with annoying-ass kids walking around and screaming for no reason. Cocky-ass teenage girls thinking they are the shit, with men salivating behind them. Then you have the ones that are just here to window shop. I thought of stopping into Bath and Body

Works... but of course, the store is jam-packed. *Nice. Is this a new lingerie store? I may need to come back this way when we are done.*

"Sis, let's go in here to see what they have." She walks toward the new lingerie store called Lady Rose Intimates. Now that's my girl!

She pulls me to the side.

"This is slightly embarrassing; however, I really need your help with finding the right outfits. I need something very hip, sexy, and defiant. Your big sister should be on point with this, but I am never good at wearing anything daring. You, on the other end, always look amazing, and this will be the first time Oscar will see me looking like a tall glass of expensive wine as opposed to my generic jogger outfit." We engage in a laugh.

"I got you, sis, come on."

CHAPTER TWELVE

I go to a nearby hotel of the restaurant to get dressed for my date with Mike, listening to Earth, Wind, and Fire and dancing around the room while preparing. Mom and Pop used to jive to these songs. Growing up, I couldn't get enough of my '50s, '60s, and '70s type of music. I tell ya, it is so much better than most of the songs that are out today.

Naz and I are having more good days than bad. His romance has stepped up a bit, and he's started to take charge. I guess with many years of begging for change, I am finally receiving the love and attention that I need. Sadly, it's after I've received love and attention from somebody else. That is awful; and what I did will always haunt me, but I can't explain what Mike does to me; he makes me lose myself. The moment I see him, I am in complete submission mode. He can tell me to do anything, and I'll do it promptly. These last few months have been astronomically amazing. I feel alive, just like my sister. Both of us are walking around with a moon-light expression, just gleaming! I turn up the music to try and block out my inner thoughts.

It is just about time for me to head out, and I'm pondering which shoes to put on. I decide to go with the nude shoes. They work well with my twist-back mini fitted darted bodice dress with a slit and cutout waist-line. I haven't dressed up in quite some time, yet this weekend I am looking more formal than usual two days in a row. It's getting close to my time, so I order the UberX. Figured an SUV would fit the look. During the wait, I go to the lobby of the hotel. Men are literally growling at me for attention. I've turned down at least six in only fifteen minutes. I guess that is a great indica-tion of how amazing I look. I've never been to this location, never even heard of it. So I decide to google it before my Uber arrives. It has a 5-star rating, and it also has a five-dollar sign symbol, which indicates that it is a pretty damn expensive location, with many great reviews. I am impressed.

The Uber arrives.

THE PARKING LOT is long and curving. A few seconds later, the restaurant comes into a clear view. It is lovely. Downlighting is cast onto the restaurant. The light shines down on it, and the landscape absolutely adds softer lighting, mimicking the moonlight. Planters and small fairy lights dress up the entrance and add an additional ambiance. It is professionally maintained. The driver pulls up to the many cars in the line of entrance. There he is—he appears in the front on the top step. His focus is on the car, and it seems as if he knows it is me, so he leans on the door with one hand in his pocket while the other hand rubs on his goatee.

The driver assists me with getting out of the car. I'm praying I won't lose balance with these shoes. The moment he spots me, he sways his way over to the car, our eyes fixated on each other. I stand, charmingly awaiting his arrival. I haven't felt butterflies or this much excitement in such a long time. He raises his eyebrows and stops about two feet from me.

"Walk toward me." I nod and do as he commanded.

He grabs my hand, rubs my palm, and then kisses my knuckles. I blush. He bites his bottom lip and motions closer to me, whispering in my ear, "You look ravishing tonight, Zadie."

"Thank you; you look very handsome, Mike. Never pictured this side of you."

He is breathtaking, dapper, and smells amazing. He's wearing a long-sleeve knitted blazer that hits his hips with dark wash denim jeans. A beaded bracelet, perforated leather lace-up shoe, with his collar popped. He grabs my waist and escorts me into the restaurant.

"Wow, this place is remarkable; I feel underdressed. How did you even find out about this place?"

He catches my breath by stopping us in our tracks, turning to me. He looks deep in my eyes, cups my chin, and feeds on my lips. I am so lost in our kiss that I slightly lose my balance as he releases me.

"You are extraordinarily breathtaking tonight. Don't ever doubt yourself." I am completely bashful. He wraps his arms around my waist as we enter the restaurant. The waiting area is full of small couches, benches, and chairs. The entrance leads right into the dining area, which creates a seamless flow.

He already has our section available. Not sure if it is VIP, but it is secluded in the far back nook by the kitchen and the wines, with a hint of privacy, but it still offers a view of everything. There is an elegant stream of service and high energy distant chattering. We are provided with two wine bottles readily available and a complimentary breadbasket, which includes a rustic French roll, a slice of raisin nut loaf bread, and a bran muffin. The waiter arrives. It takes me longer than normal to order, as they have so many amazing options.

"I am just going to run into the little boys' room; I'll be right back, sweetheart."

I acknowledge. I guess while I wait, I should open this bottle of red wine. Soft music is playing in the midst of the restaurant.

"Oh, forgive me, this is the wrong section." A young lady accidentally walks into my VIP section. "Oh my God, Zadie, is that you?"

Holy shit! This is not fucking happening right now! An uncomfortable pause comes before me.

"Heeeeey, you. How is everything?" I say with an obviously uneasy and rattled expression.

"I am doing well. What are you doing all the way on the west side? You are pretty far from home. Is your husband here?" *Think, think, think, Zadie*!!

"No, he is not. I am with my sister and her friend, who just lost someone dear to her. We took her out to ease her mind a bit."

"That is so nice of you two to be there for a friend during this rough time. Well, good to see you. Give your husband best wishes for me. Let me head out; I finally located my girlfriend. Sorry again for the inconvenience and startling you."

"Please don't worry about it; you are perfectly fine. Enjoy the rest of your night."

I quickly chug back my glass of wine. I am so fucked!! This is a sign I shouldn't be here; I need to go. I grab my purse to run out, but I am stopped in my tracks.

"Whoa, you damn near knocked me down, baby. Are you okay…? You were not about to run out on me, were you?"

"Mike, I'm so dizzy right now," I say as I grab on to him to maintain my balance.

"Hey, hey, come here, baby." He helps me sit down and sits next to me.

"You are quivering uncontrollably, baby, talk to me. What just happened? What did I miss? Did someone say something to you?"

He holds me tight while my head is planted on his chest as he softly rubs his fingers across my nape. I am crying and shaking with fear. I'm going to lose everything. I know she's going to say something to him.

"Talk to me." He softly lifts my head from his chest, kisses every teardrop, then rubs my face gently with a linen napkin.

"Look at me… Relax… Let's take a deep breath together… and again…"

"Okay, her husband works out at the same boxing

ring that my husband works out at, and she's there with her husband fifty percent of the time. I know this because I am there fifty percent of the time during my school breaks. She accidentally looked in this booth while she was looking for her girlfriend. I lied and told her I was with one of my friends who just lost someone, but I don't think she bought it. I feel like she's going to say something to my husband... This is wrong, Mike; this is so wrong." My tears start to fall again.

"I understand this is frightening for you, but what's done is done, and there is nothing you can do about it now. If she decides to say anything to your husband, you leaving at this point wouldn't matter. You go to school on the west, don't you? This is a piece of cake for you; just tell him the same exact story you told her. The difference would be you came here right after class."

"Since you put it that way, I guess I can go with that."

"As hard as it is for me to say this, if you feel it is best to go, then we will leave. What do you wish to do?"

He rubs his fingers through my hair.

I exhale, then place my head on his broad shoulders, landing sweet kisses on his neck. His cologne tickles my nose.

I feel him release the tension from his chest since that indicated I'm not going anywhere.

I pour us each a glass of wine.

"Mike, I don't know you. I don't know what you *really* do for a living, if you have children, siblings. I don't know anything about you, yet oddly enough, your presence makes me whole. It can simply be because I'm lonely, vulnerable, and I gave you the opportunity to take it this far. As a married woman, I should not have, but what's done is done as you say. Yet I ask myself, do I really need to know all of that? Do I really need to get further involved with you?"

"Why do you think we are here, Zadie? I'm ready to have that *talk* with you… Don't get me wrong; I definitely thought the same. Should we really get that involved with each other? Being that you are married I can't expect too much. Then I thought to myself I'd rather get let down than to let you go."

The waiter comes back and asks if we are ready for our entree at this time. When I was going through my emotional fit, the waiter came by, and Mike told him to leave. But I am starving right now, and a girl can definitely eat.

After dinner, we talk for nearly two hours. I find out that he is a widower; his wife passed away three years ago while giving birth to their child, and unfortunately, their child didn't make it. I am so heartbroken by that story. He doesn't have any other children. He is a hard worker. He is also a part of his family business. They run an architectural firm in Nassau county. They've been in business for nearly 32 years, which explains how an electrician has a yacht. Business seems to be going pretty well. He has a younger sister that lives somewhere in the five boroughs; they don't have much of a relationship, but he'll do anything for her. His father passed several years ago, which changed his life. He and his mother have an amazing relationship, and she is dying for some grandkids.

My life isn't as exciting, but I tell him the gist of it —my parents passing and how my sister and I are very close. I also tell him about the date that all of us will be going on tomorrow. We laugh about sis finally dating. We have a great time.

I take a sip of my water and look at the time.

"Guess I should call my ride now?"

"Don't be silly; I'll drive you. I'll pay on our way out."

"I can help with the bill. Dutch style."

He chuckles.

"Dutch style? You are adorable; let's go. I got this now and always. You'll never have to worry about going into your pockets."

He circles his finger over my knuckles. We are on our feet at this time. His eyes glitter as he stands before me. He is a mere breath from my lips. He wraps his arms around me, searching my eyes.

"You are someone very important to me; you know that, don't you?"

"I never wanted more joy until I met you. I am quite taken with you."

He has one arm around me, clutching me to him while his thumb traces my exposed waistline. "Let's go." He grabs my hands and leads the way out of the restaurant.

We wait for the valet to bring his car.

A few cars arrive at the front of the restaurant.

"This is mine." We walk toward an emblem green Mercedes-Benz wagon.

"A G-Class I see."

"You know your cars."

I shrug.

"A little something, something."

He opens the door and assists me into the wagon. This car is exquisitely crafted. You are immediately greeted with an elaborate multizone LED ambient lighting system with slowly changing hues, contoured front seats, large display that seems to be primarily controlled through a rotary knob, and a touchpad mounted on the center console. He enters the car. I think my stare startles him.

"What, what is that inquisitive look about?" His eyes squint.

"You are a drug dealer, aren't you? You better get me out of this car, Mike!"

He laughs and peers at me.

"I did not say anything funny, Mike." I sit there with my arms around me like a child, trying to hold in my laugh.

He laughs even louder. "You are adorable when you pout. Is it because of the car?"

"The wagon, to be exact, yes, that is the reason. Be honest with me, please."

"Sweetcakes, I will never put you in danger, you hear me, and don't you ever forget that. I am not who you think I am."

I lower my eyes and start toying with my purse. I've never seen him this stern.

"We had a good night, sweetcakes, we sat for hours, and I told you what I do full-time as well as part-time. My family business has been very good to me throughout the years that I took over… I have a yacht, but why is this car the deal breaker for you?"

He is right…I struggle to respond. I take a deep breath, then turn to face him. "I mean, technically, I shouldn't care, I am literally nobody to you," I murmur.

He is staring into my eyes, his nostrils flared. Chest tightened, he closes his eyes and takes a deep breath.

"What the heck, Zadie? A quick-witted woman like yourself came up with that response? You're right; you mean shit to me."

He peels off, driving erratically. We drive in silence and absolute tension. I don't know what to say, so it's best to not say anything at all.

He pulls up in front of the hotel. I hastily get out of the car. He gets out as well and quickly runs after me and grabs my wrist.

"Don't touch me!" I say with a strong, loud, clear shout.

"What are you doing?" he whispers. "Zadie, you are the one that created this cloud between us. We had an amazing night that could've stayed afloat, and you killed it with your accusations and smart comments. You know you mean more to me than a piece of ass."

"I don't know that at all. I am a married woman, I belong to someone else, there is absolutely nothing more that you need from me but sex…"

He looks at me with a perplexed expression.

"This must be the alcohol. Are you drunk? This isn't the person that I know."

"Mike, YOU DON'T KNOW ME at all, and I don't know you; there is nothing more that we can do at this point but just to walk away from each other!"

He just stands there, gawping at me. I peer at my watch, then walk into the hotel without saying another word. I take one glance back, but he is gone. I open the door to my room, take off my shoes, flop onto the bed, and glare at the ceiling. Mike was right; I am mortified by my behavior. I was using my feeling of guilt and taking it out on him. However, the way we left it tonight is for the best. Though I didn't think it was going to hurt this much... I go to the bathroom, shower, cry, and get myself together to head home.

Phone chimes: message from Mike

Are you on your way home?

It's best to just delete his message and keep it moving.

CHAPTER THIRTEEN

"Hey, baby Z. Where have you been all night? I've called a few times." Naz is sunk down on the couch watching boxing, of course. I go to him and sit on his lap as tears flow down. I can't hold it in anymore, and as usual, I go into a bawling fit.

"Baby, what's on your mind?" His eyes are brimming with concern. He turns off the television.

"Zamora, Kelle, and I went for dinner and drinks directly after class. My friend lost her husband. We took her out to assist with easing her pain. Naz, I can't imagine losing you. I'd die."

I've twisted the lie just a tad.

"I'm sorry to hear about your friend, baby. I really hope she had a good time tonight."

"I believe she did. But I'm exhausted. I'm going to jump in the shower, then head to bed, baby. Will you join me?" I state seductively in his ear.

"Is that a new perfume you're wearing?" He glances at me speculatively.

Shit! My heart is pounding. I am sure he is refencing Mike's cologne. I forgot to replace my neckerchief. I struggle to answer the question. "Something like that. It was actually a sample. The restaurant was near a mall, and you know how they love to test spray the public."

Much to my relief, I think he buys that. Once we are done small talking, I head to the shower.

I have eight text messages from Mike inquiring if I made it home safe and how he was disappointed with how the night ended.

Hi. I made it safe, I'm well. I hope you are doing well yourself.

I wait a few minutes for him to respond.

I was beginning to worry Zadie! When will I see you again?

Mike, I'm not sure if that's a good idea. I have to go. Good night.

I turn off my phone, then head to the shower…

CHAPTER FOURTEEN

"Zamora, we are going to be late for our hair and nail appointment. Let's go already!" After sitting in my car for 20 minutes, I decide to run into sis's house to grab breakfast. One thing about Zamora, she loves her breakfast. She is always throwing it down in the kitchen.

"Okay, okay, hold your horses. Maybe if you help with the dishes, things will move a lot quicker."

"Well, maybe if you help with my schoolwork from time to time, things will move much quicker."

We laugh.

"I am heading outside, lingerer. Maybe that'll assist with putting some pep in your step."

"GOSH, I hate traffic. Why must I always drive, Zadie?"

"Big sisters always take the wheel. It is the best thing since sliced bread."

"You are terrible= what does that even mean? You and these damn idioms, where do you get them from? They make absolutely no sense at all," Zamora says as she snickers.

"Soooo spill the beans... Did you and Oscar....?"

"No, no, and no. Trust me, I am yearning for him! Maybe tonight, hence why I bought the lingerie."

"Gosh, Zamora, how long has it been?"

"To tell you the truth, I lost track. Maybe close to three years. I can't explain how nervous I am."

"Zamora, you will be fine; I hope he truly rocks your boat tonight or whenever you two decide to take it a step further!"

"Oh, I strongly believe he will in fact rock this raggedy-ass boat. I do not doubt that at all."

"Sis! On a wider spectrum, I can't believe you took my advice and cut your hair; it fits you so well. Oscar and Naz will be so surprised."

Sis is such a bore. Her hairstyles have been outdated since the '80s. I've been telling her for years to change her hairdo.

"I'm surprised that I actually like it."

"Of course you do. You look amazing."

We are done with our daily runs. Our hair and nails are on point, and we are ready for the night.

"Well, Zamora, this is me, thanks for the ride. I'll see you in a few hours. We'll meet you guys there."

"Wait, we are not getting dressed together?"

"Were we supposed to?"

"Yes, I just assumed you'd help me get right with my outfit, makeup, the whole bit."

"Of course, I'll be happy to! So you'll bring your things to my house?"

"Yes, even though the location is out in the city, I don't mind driving out to you to get right."

"Okay, cool, be there at 9, and *PLEASE* don't be late, Ms. Tardiness."

"I got you, Zadie. I'll be there at 8."

"Whatever, just be there by 9 or before."

WHEN I ARRIVE HOME, Naz is not there. I suppose he is getting his shit together for tonight. Mike has been blowing up my phone all day. I really want to respond, but this decision is more than likely going to stick. He seems to be such a great man, but I love my husband, and I'm going to try and fix our demons. They always say the third time is the charm.

I am so excited about tonight; it is literally the first night in so long that my sister and I are going out on a double date. I don't know if I'm more excited because she's going to look amazing or because she's going to get some buns tonight. Well, I guess a mixture of both.

"Hey, baby."

I am startled as Naz walks behind me while I am doing my hair.

"Hey, baby, gosh, you scared me. What, why are you giving me that look?"

"I love you with my life; you know that, don't you?"

"Of course, baby." I take a deep breath, closing my eyes.

"Kiss me." Naz grabs the back of my neck and gracefully kisses me. While our tongues are intertwined, we walk over to the sofa. I am only in my T-shirt and panties; he grabs both breasts and begins to bite gently on each nipple. I grab the back of his head, bringing him deeper into my breasts. He bends me over the sofa, spreads my legs, and goes to work on my pussy from behind while fingering my ass. I am completely engulfed in his pleasure.

After I made the confession about the affair, his sexual juices were flowing. From daily sex in the shower, inside movie theaters, eating my twat, and tossing my salad. Whatever you can think of, he was absolutely doing. He made sure that I was pleased. It is just so terrible that after my affair admission was when he changed. I guess that is a normal reaction.

We sit on the couch for about an hour, just kicking it. No TV, phones, laptops, nothing, just all conversation. I feel satisfied for cutting things off with Mike; he was a different kind of man, very rough, but sweet at the same time. I can't say I'll stay with him for the money. My Naz makes excellent money and is very supportive as I continue my education.

"I am very ecstatic about tonight. What did you get to wear?" I place my head on his leg.

"You'll see soon enough, baby Z," Naz states while grinning as we both giggle.

"Well, we had a nice long talk, but now I must prepare myself before sis arrives."

Sis arrives. "Hey, Nazzir! Come give your sis a hug."

Naz and sis are straight-up cool as hell! At one point, I felt he was closer to her than he was with me. I asked him not to share personal information with her, which I do not believe he does. Sis would have sat me down a long time ago or slapped me due to my affair.

While they are still hugging, she says, "Naz, I need

your advice. Did sis tell you about Oscar, my new boo thang?"

"A lil something something. Why, what's up?"

"It has been a few months, and he asked me to move in with him."

"WHAT!?" I holler from the kitchen. "You didn't tell me that, sis, we were together all day yesterday!"

"He just asked me last night."

"Then, in that case, you call me and wake me up at 2 in the damn morning! What kind of shit is this?"

"Sorry, sis. I figured I'd seek advice from you *and* Naz."

"Nah, you only asked Naz, I was in the kitchen!"

"Sis, come on. No need to bicker, but I really do need y'all advice."

"I'll say do it, you only live once, and sis, if you do not jump on this, you might be single for another five years." They both erupt in laughter.

"NO, I disagree! You only knew this guy for what, a few months? This is purely the superficial stage, where y'all only tell each other what the other wants to hear. You may be jumping the gun here. By any means, I am not telling you to do something out of the normal, but small things, such as cutting your hair, or getting something sexy to wear, or even going to meet his parents.

But don't start this off doing wife duties at girlfriend price."

My sis just stands there with her brows raised. Her voice cracks as if she is a few moments away from getting emotional.

"I take it that you don't approve. Thanks, sis," she states sarcastically.

"Well, my wife dropped the mic, I slightly agree, but again you only live once. If he is serious about it, he'll wait for you."

She gains more control over her voice. "I understand you both, and I just wanted your opinion," she says as she walks her way to the sitting area.

"Sis, don't leave like that. You know I will always keep it real with you. It doesn't make sense to be upset with me. Ultimately it is your decision; I will support you either way."

"I know, guys; I won't move in with him. Not yet. I know it was way too soon; I just needed to hear it from someone else. Anyway, enough about that, how about we get ready? I am eager to see him!"

"Sounds about right. Let's do this!"

We go to the second level of the house to get ready while listening to Jay-Z "School of Hard Knocks."

CHAPTER FIFTEEN

We are done getting ready. We walk down my spiral staircase heading toward the door, looking stunning. Naz and is standing at the end, awaiting our arrival.

Naz can't take his eyes off of me. Zamora's body in her dress is flawless. She has on a very snugged, sleeveless, light brown deep v neck bodycon midi dress. She paired the dress with a red strappy heel and a stylish clutch bag for a gorgeous full body look. It has been such a long time since I've actually gone out with my sister this excited. It is driving me insane.

"My ladies, you two look amazing." Naz comes in very close to me, inhaling my scent.

As for me, I have on a red, deep v neck, long sleeve floral lace midi dress with a bodysuit under, paired with a furry white crop coat, white pumps, bold necklace along with a mini crossbody bag, and RayBan shades.

"But you, you look delicious." He grabs my hand and places it on his dick. My eyes widen.

"No way!!! I haven't felt him in so long," I whisper. "We'll be right back, sis!"

I grab Naz's hand and run to the bedroom. I don't care about my clothes or hair; I just want to make love to my husband before his dick turns flat! After his injury, he has been stuck on these medications that also do nerve damage, which doesn't allow him to even get an erection. I want to take full advantage of what is happening right now.

We don't even make it to the bed. I grab his face with my hands as I roughly kiss him. He turns me around, my hands flat on top of the ottoman bench. He props one leg on the ottoman and fucks me crazy from behind. He sounds like a damn grizzly bear; I have to place my panties in his mouth to muffle the sound so that Zamora will not hear us. As he fucks me like crazy, I can feel his balls hitting my clit as my juices flow down my inner thighs.

I then sit on the edge of the ottoman, quickly turn around, and plunge his dick in and out of my mouth. He is fucking my mouth back so hard that I gag a few times. He then sits on the edge of the bed, and I straddle him, fucking him like crazy. I go to work on his dick, from in my pussy, then back in my mouth, in my pussy, then back in my mouth. I then turn around and begin to fuck him cowgirl style. He grabs my waist and lifts me while his dick is still in me. He is now on top of me, licking my whole body from head to toe.

"I forgot how good *she she* felt." Yeah, he has a name for my pussy, aka she she!

He pounds me till we come in unison; I am more than certain Zamora heard us. We are lying there, breathing heavily, staring at each other as he gently kisses me on my forehead.

"You are still amazing, baby Z."

"And you are still my beast. I love you. We must shower, and I'd love for you to join me." He smiles and nods, and we arrive downstairs as fresh as we were an hour ago.

"Freaks, we are late, and my man is waiting for me," says Zamora while laughing.

"Shut up, and let's go." We are cracking up.

THE SPOT IS ABSOLUTELY JUMPING; you can hear the music nearly one block from the location. The valet takes our car.

Oscar is waiting outside for us to arrive. Our men are looking dapper! Naz has on white trousers, a light blue shirt, and a navy blazer with a printed pocket square and black leather oxford dress shoes. Oscar is wearing indigo denim, a light blue shirt, gray blazer, and a navy tie with tan dress shoes. When Zamora gets out of the car, Oscar looks at her just as she wanted him to, like a nice tall glass of wine. There is no one in sight but Zamora; it looks like Oscar floated on water to get to her. I actually cry; my sister is finally happy with a man that treats her remarkably. I love everything about this relationship.

"Hey, Oscar, you clean up nice! Good to see you again. Please meet the love of my life, my husband, Nazzir."

They greet, then we make our way into the club. The club is packed, with a captivating theatrical sophisticated nightlife atmosphere.

This is one of the hottest clubs in NYC. We are VIP, so we enter through our own private entrance located next to the right of the lounge.

The best way to describe the crowd is upscale fashionable. I don't see hats, sandals, flip-flops, sneakers, work boots, shorts, baggy clothing, or athletic wear. Purely upscale. As we make our way to the table, the dance floor is lit up.

The DJ is playing the best music out. Once we make it to the table, we have our designated bartender, who offers bottle service of vodka and tequila. The bottles have flashing LED lights. It includes a cart or tray of mixers, club soda, ginger ale, cola, cranberry juice, limes, and lemons, with a mix of fresh-squeezed blood orange juice.

Zamora, is extremely uncomfortable and nervous, so she quickly takes a swig of tequila. Obviously to relax, and I give her another and another. By the fifth shot two hours later, she is in the corner grinding hard on Oscar. *That's my girl!* On the other side, Naz and I are going at it on the dance floor like we are two horny 17-year-olds. I am gyrating my hips on his dick through his trousers, rubbing, licking, moaning, kissing, touching, you name it! An odd feeling tells me to turn around as I feel this unknown presence, and there he is, looking as scrumptious as he could, wearing a gray wool overcoat, dark gray crew neck tee, gray trousers, and gray scarf with black shoes. *Mike* is just standing there staring at us with a glass of wine. I immediately lose my balance.

"Baby, you are drunk, shall we sit for a while?"

"Maybe a bit tipsy, not drunk. But I will take a seat. As a matter of fact, you know what, baby, I need to run to the ladies' room. I will be right back."

My eyes are full of fury. I don't take my eyes off of Mike while walking to the restroom so that he is aware to follow me. I am not in the mood for his bullshit. I stand around the corner, waiting for his arrival. The moment he turns the corner, I brace up on him.

"Are you fucking following me?"

He undresses me with his eyes. "Damn, girl, you look good," he says as he touches my ass.

"Get your hands off of me!"

"So it is like that. All I want to do is be with you. I was annoyed and pissed off that you were ignoring my calls and texts. I didn't know what else to do, Zadie. I am falling for you, Z. I know I shouldn't feel this way, but I do, and there is nothing I can do about it. I really don't want to cause any issues with you and your husband. Just tell me to leave and move on, and I will."

Damn! This is so confusing! Why did I get myself in this deep shit! Staring at his puppy eyes just fucking melts me, always! He has just pulled me back into his realm.

"Leave me the hell alone, Mike. Did I make myself clear?"

"Do you mean that Z? Do you really mean that?" He pulls in closer to me.

How, how did I get myself so deep into this? I can

cry just with the thought of letting him go, and I do just that—sob!

"Hey, hey, don't do that, baby." He walks up to me and cradles my head in his chest. I have been away from my husband for just about ten minutes. I should be heading back; I am so captivated by his aura—not to mention that he smells and looks so divine!

I slowly made my way to his neck and plant soft kisses, whispering, "I don't want to lose you, Mike, but I am just so confused, scared, and married, but I do have to go. I will text you." It takes me a minute or two to realize what I am doing, then I abruptly back away quickly with hopes my sister, Oscar, or my husband didn't catch me.

"I have to go."

"Nah, not until I am done."

"Mike, please stop and let go of me. I really have to go." I don't think my cries are taken seriously.

He abruptly drags me out the back door of the club, not too far from the restrooms. He closes the door, picks me up, and wraps my legs around his waist, holding me up against the door. He pulls my breast out from my V-neck dress and begins to suck on my left nipple.

"I miss you so much," he whispers, now sucking gently on my earlobe while putting on his condom.

"This is for me, Zadie. I'll make it quick." He grabs both of my ass cheeks, pulling me in closer so that I can feel his dick so deep inside of me, pounding me. The dude fucks me like I've never imagined. I don't want him to stop. I feel him come as his dick throbs inside of me. We stand there for a moment. I slide my body down from off the door.

"I need to get inside. I will text you."

While I am getting myself together, walking back into the club, I see *my husband...* watch us walk inside the club from the backdoor. *Holy shit.*

The expression on his face says it all. Mike and I stand by the doorway, looking at Naz in complete shock.

"What the fuck is going on, Zadie?" he asks while he walks toward us. I am lost for words.

"What the fuck is going on, Zadie!?" he says louder. "Who is this motherfucker?" He is aggressively pointing to Mike.

"Nobody, baby, just someone I know." Before I know it, he charges toward Mike, but I intervene. "NAZ STOP, PLEASE!"

"Is this the dude you're fucking, Zadie? I know how you look after I fuck your brains out, and that is exactly how you looked when you walked in here."

He charges at us again. This time, he grabs my hair

and swings me to the ground. He drags me on the floor, literally through the club, right out the front door. I am screaming for help, but no one helps me. I can hear Mike trying to stop him, but others are holding him back. My husband has that much pull and muscle at the club due to who he is; they corner Mike and allow him to do as he pleases.

"ZAMORA!" I scream, but she doesn't come for me. We finally make it to the car. He beats the shit out of me in the backseat of the car with his belt that cuts into my body. The pain is so excruciating that I sleep in the backseat from exhaustion...

CHAPTER SIXTEEN

The sun is hitting my face. I am in my guestroom bed, showered, with my night slip on. I get up, but instantly feel the pain of welts on my body. I walk out of the bedroom; the smell of eggs hits my nose. It takes me longer to get to the kitchen due to the pain. While walking to the kitchen, I see it is minutes past 11 am. My sis and Oscar are there. I am standing in the middle of the room looking at everybody, like…. was last night all a fucking dream!? How is my sister just laughing with this dick?

"Hey, sleepyhead, we heard you couldn't handle your liquor last night. You were vomiting on everyone and had to leave suddenly," Zamora states while giving me a hug. I have to brace from the pain in my back. I stare at Naz like I can spit fire!

"So that's what he told you happened, huh, sis?"

"Zamora, can you please finish these eggs? I am going to give Zadie a pill that'll help her recover from this hangover. Come on, baby." He grabs my hand, but I pull back and follow him upstairs.

He closes the door behind him, then begins to pace the floor. He drops on his knees, places his head on my legs, and begins to sob. "There are no words to say that will make up for my reaction last night."

I stand there like a zombie just staring in dead air, listening to this weakling. He is talking, but I'm not listening. One thing I do know, I need to leave his ass, but I have to plan my departure strategically. I have a little over a year for school. But he can pay for the year in two months when registration reopens. I will not stand for a man physically abusing me! Yes, I know I was trifling by what I've done, but I never ever in my life thought Naz would abuse me! Back to reality....

"Baby, answer me, do you understand?"

"Yup."

By this time, he is standing in front of me.

"I think we should get back downstairs to our company; I didn't share any of this information with your sister, just so you know."

I nod. Of course he didn't. My sister would be in handcuffs!

"I will be down in a min."

He walks out of the room, then peeks his head back in.

"Don't think about going on your phone; it's broken. The new phone should arrive tomorrow." He proceeds downstairs.

This fucking bastard! I sneak into my study and check my email. Lo and behold, there are tons of emails from Mike. The last one was seven minutes ago.

Baby, If anything happened to you, I swear to god!

Hey baby, I am not okay! This asshole beat me with a belt, Mike! I have welts all over my body! What happened to you last night? I blacked out. Anyway, he killed my phone. I won't be able to reach out to you till I am near my computer, which is often due to school work. But I am not sure when I'll see you again. I don't want to see you like this. I will stick with emails for now. I am in so much pain; I wish I was with you. I am so sorry; I got you into this mess. Just know, I started falling for you too. I didn't know how to love two people at one time. Please hit me back.

I go back into the guestroom, really not wanting to

be bothered with anyone. I take two pain relievers and go back to sleep. By the time I wake up, it is 9 pm. I go into the kitchen to get a glass of water.

Naz is sleeping, and sis has left me a note on my nightstand.

Naz told me you broke your phone last night, and he ordered another one today for you. So, I guess we will talk tomorrow. You didn't look well, I guess, due to the hangover. I hope you are feeling much better by the time you wake up. I missed you today, and last night, I was so twisted last night. But, girl! After some light hesitancy on my end, he rocked my damn world last night, my legs are still trembling!! I will tell you all about it in our next gathering! I love you, baby sis! Get well, and call me from the house or Naz phone when you wake.

Thankfully, Naz left me dinner because I am starving. I prepare a bath as I need to soak my body. I decide to make a spa for myself. I light candles, play some slow jams, get my laptop, then place it on the bathroom caddy tub tray. Before logging into my email, I relax for about 30 minutes in peppermint and frankincense oil.

What the fuck, Zadie! He put his hands on you! Good thing about having a professional boxer as your husband, your address is easy to obtain. I'm on my way....

I damn near drop the caddy on the floor. I hop out of the tub as quickly as if I wasn't in pain. He sent the email close to an hour ago; if anything, he's here already, but maybe he is bluffing. I put my robe on and run to the front door; I notice his green wagon sitting four houses down from my house. *Oh my God, oh my God, oh my God.* I run to the car with nothing on my feet and just a robe on. I quietly close the door and turn off the lights so it looks like I am sleeping.

He's out of the car with a bat in his hands.

"Get in the car right now, Mike, right now!" I sternly whisper.

"Where is he, where's that bastard husband of yours?"

"Keep your voice down, please, and get in the car!"

He pushes me out of the way.

"Ouch, Mike, I told you I am in so much pain. You

come here upsetting me and getting me more emotional for what? To stand out here with a bat. I don't need this agitation from you. I'm going through so much in my home right now; I can't take more pain!"

"I am on edge right now, but you're right, baby, I'm sorry, but just the thought of someone abusing you, a sweet soul like you just really pissed me off."

I get into his car and close the door. He looks back at me, and after several minutes with a calm demeanor, he gets into the car as well.

He holds my hand, and we sit quietly. "How bad did he hurt you?"

I pull off my robe and turn around so he can look at my bruised back.

He clenches his jawbone and flares his nostrils. I place my hand on his chest, and I can feel his heart pounding.

"Mike, I really don't want to talk about this right now. I was taking a nice relaxing bath when I read your email and ran outside; my whole entire body hurts. I wish I could just wake up from this nightmare."

"It seemed as if your husband had some type of pull last night because of who he is. When he grabbed you, I went toward him; however, several men blocked me, threw me out the back door, and locked me out. I ran my way to the front entrance after hopping over fences, but you were already gone. I was beyond furious, not knowing what happened to you or where you were, but as bittersweet as this moment is, I'm glad you're doing okay."

"I am so sorry I got you involved in this mess." Tears begin to flow.

"I never imagined that he'd hit me. This is beyond low. This is our mess, and I don't regret meeting you at all. You have changed my life, and this is a prime example."

I chuckle a little.

"Glad to see a smile on your face. Come home with me. Don't worry about your clothes, just come home with me."

"Mike, as tempting as that sounds, you know that I can't."

"Don't tell me that you plan on staying with him after all of this!"

"I never said that! I need time, that's all. I have to figure shit out. Get a new place, file for divorce, it's just not an easy pick-up and go. Then I have school to worry about."

"Zadie, he is not the only dude with money. Whatever you need, school, wardrobe, place to stay, I got you!"

"That's very sweet of you, and I will take you up on

that offer, just give me some time, Mike. I'm sorry, but I really have to get back inside before he realizes I'm gone."

"How do you expect me to sleep knowing that you are not sleeping easy? That you have to sleep with one eye open?"

"I'm going inside to finish my bath. I'll email you in the process. You can leave; I'll be okay. If you don't hear from me in two days, then worry. I'll email you my sister's number. However, please only use it for emergencies."

I can see this didn't sit well with him, but there is nothing I can do at this point. He's going to have to accept it and keep it moving at least for now...

"Do you mind if I sit here and wait for your email so that I will know you are okay?"

"Absolutely."

"Come here."

He leans in and plants a soft kiss on my lips and runs his fingers through my damp hair.

"Email me as soon as you get back inside." He grabs my chin. "You understand me?"

I nod.

I get out of the car and go into the house.

"Where are you coming from?" Oh hell! He is

standing by the door in the dark; what the hell is he was doing!?

"I went to take a look at…the garden. I thought I heard a possum back there." It feels like I've been holding my breath for 40 minutes.

"You shouldn't walk outside barefoot, baby."

I can't stop shaking.

"I am going to take a shower; I'll see you in a few."

I go back to the bathroom, take a quick shower to remove the dirt off my body, and then restart my bath.

I am okay, he was by the door omg I was so scared, but I am fine! Seriously I am fine, back in the tub.

As long as you are okay, then I am good; try to email me as much as you can. I am heading out.

I make my way out of the tub and into my guestroom to get dressed.

"Who were you with in that car, Zadie?"

He comes up behind me with his hands around my neck, practically choking me.

"A wagon, to be exact!" I knee him in his dick, and while he's hunched over, I knee him in his head. He falls backward on to the floor. I run out of the room into our room, grab the gun safe from the top shelf of the closet, and enter the pin. I go back into the room and hold the gun to his face.

"If you ever put your hands on me again, I will fucking kill you, do you hear me?"

"Oh, shit. Oh, damn baby, you really going to shoot me?" He crawls into a corner as I follow him with the pistol to his head.

"SHUT UP and answer my question! Did you hear me?"

"Yes, yes. I. Did," he says, scared and trembling, his hands outstretched toward the gun. There is a look of death in my eyes and fear in his.

"You aren't really going to shoot me, Zadie, me, your husband, the love of your life, are you?"

"You dragged me through a crowded upscale club by my hair, beat me with a leather belt in the backseat of our car in front of that same club til I welted, and choked me. Do you really want me to think of you as the love of my life right now, Nazzir?"

"I fucked up, iight, I fucked up, but you fucked up too, Zadie! You out there fucking on me! You told me you were going to stop! Tell me you didn't fuck that nigga in that back alley of the club Zadie, WHILE I WAS THERE?"

"SHUT UP!"

My palms are sweaty, and my knees are buckling. I

am a nervous wreck holding this gun to my husband's head. I have no idea who this girl is right now; it is totally out of character. He is right; I fucked up big time, which still doesn't give him the right to abuse me in any aspect. I am emotionally torn.

"Baby, baby, look at me. Look at me. Is this what we've come to, you holding a gun to my head?"

I gradually begin to lower my arms to place the gun down. I can't hold my emotions steady, so I break down and fall to my knees. He kicks the gun away from us and cradles me in his arms.

"I don't know what to do; I am so lost," I whimper.

"We'll get through this, baby; I will make sure of that. I'll never hit you again."

I've never felt so far away from him. He is not the man I once knew.

CHAPTER SEVENTEEN

The sun rose, but I don't want to get out of bed. Not sure where Naz went, and neither do I care. I am sure by this time, Mike is looking for my morning email. I'm just not up for that as well. I just want to seclude myself in a closet and not move for a full day. Heal and think of my next move. Tomorrow, I will check out the online used car sites to get my own car. That will be my first step.

"Good, you are up. Wish to talk about what happened last night?"

I wrap my body in the sheets and face the option direction. He stands at the edge of the bed; I can feel his stare.

"So that is how we now do things, Zadie. I am sorry, I am so sorry for being an asshole. I am sorry for putting my hand on you. I am sorry for embarrassing you, us, and our marriage."

He crawls into the bed under the sheets and holds me. Holds me tight, whispering in my ear, "I can't lose you, I can't, and I won't. You are my last breath. Can you turn around and look at me?"

"I need to shower, Naz; I will be back." Dude has fucked up my whole day to relax. I get up and go to shower; unfortunately, he joins me. Oddly enough, it is actually very relaxing. He massages the same welts he placed on my body with a small massage tool. He is trying to talk to me, yet he isn't getting the feedback he would like. He has a mountain to move if he thinks I am going to give in that easily. He needs to leave me be. I love him, but sorry just won't cut it. He assists with moisturizing my body and dressing me, then I go back to bed.

"Baby, do you need anything from outside? I am heading out for a short time."

"I don't need anything, Naz, thank you." The moment he leaves, I go into my study to check my emails.

As I thought, Mike has sent several emails.

Hey Mike, all is well, for now. Sorry, I took some time to email you; he was hoarding me all morning, trying to make up for the bull shit he did. I am not going for it! I am done! He is a douchebag! Anyway, the phone should arrive sometime today. I'm not sure, what the premise of the new phone might be; he may have added some type of spyware, GPS, etc. secretly installed in it. So, at this time, I feel safe, just emailing. Just remember it will take some time to hit you back; please do not panic. Two days is when you worry. Have a great day. Hope to see you soon. If I can, I promise, I will email you any opportunity I get. Ttyl

IT'S BEEN several weeks since I've seen Mike. We haven't seen each other since the incident that took place at the club—just email. Naz has been playing me much closer than normal. I am barely keeping up with my personal life, I haven't seen my sister in weeks, and I am not making my normal grades in school. I am barely sleeping, as it's been so frightening to sleep next to my husband.

It is such a beautiful day outside, and since I am unable to leave the house much, the backyard is my escape. Fresh air, my book, and nature are all I need on certain days. We have a slim hammock that I'll relax in while staring at the inground swimming pool surrounded by a sun-dappled garden and covering of trees. Time goes by so quickly, and it feels as if I have been out here for 20 minutes, which turned into four hours!

Naz pulls in the driveway. "Let's grab a few things from the market. You need to cook tonight. I am tired of fucking fast food and microwavable dishes."

I am far from being in the damn mood to go shopping. I was in a relaxed spa day mode! I don't want to even take my glasses off to look at him. I rest my head back down and ignore him.

"Zadie, did you hear me?" I hear footsteps approaching.

"Zadie?"

"I don't want to go, Naz, is that okay?"

He throws me off the hammock. I lie there staring at him.

"What the fuck was that for, Nazzir?" I scream.

"Lower your God damn voice before the neighbors hear us."

"WHY? BECAUSE YOU DON'T WANT THEM TO KNOW YOU ARE A WEAK COWARD THAT ABUSES HIS WIFE!" I am sure they can't hear me, but it is worth a try!

He quickly drags me behind the patio bar, throws

me on the floor, stands over me, and places his hands around my neck.

"Are you out of your fucking mind, Zadie?"

"No, I am sorry," are the only words I am able to screech out. The side of my face is planted on the floor. Before I know it, he has peeled my robe and lingerie back and rammed his dick inside of me. I am surprised he was even able to get a hard-on. I guess abusing me turns him on.

He fucks me hard, very hard, and since I'm not enjoying it, his dick keeps cutting my pussy. His strokes become deeper and faster. I can't even cry anymore; I close my eyes and tolerate the pain. A few times, I try to crawl away from him, but he just keeps pulling me back deeper. "Aaah!" I can no longer hold in my screams of pain. He stops…

His big ass is lying on top of me, breathing heavily. He finally gets up and pulls up his pants.

"Now, Zadie, get the fuck in the car so we can get to the market. Then you are going to come back home and cook. Isn't that right, baby Z?"

I nod, then scurry into the house, change my clothes, then we go straight to the market.

CHAPTER EIGHTEEN

"Oh, my. Please forgive me; I am all over the place today," I say as I wipe tears from my eyes and respond bashfully.

"Don't worry about it; we all have our days. You don't seem well. Is everything okay?" We're both standing in the middle of the market aisle.

I glance up to gain a full vision of the individual who had this sexy, strong, but yet sensual voice. There he is, a fine chocolate guy with smooth, toned skin standing before me. When my eyes finally meet his, I realize how scrumptious this man really is. His teeth are perfect; his brown eyes shine bright. His haircut is on point. My eyes flutter as I smile nervously at this gorgeous man.

I attempt to answer but am succumbed by a frightening expression as I glare at the gentleman standing behind him.

"I'm sorry, but I must go." I instantly run to my husband.

The gentleman turns around and witnesses Nazzir abruptly grabbing my arm.

"Let's go now," Nazzir states as his jealousy gets the best of him.

"My man, is it necessary for you to handle your Queen in that manner?"

"Mind your motherfucking business, my guy, and let me handle my fucking wife the way I want. Now let's move," Nazzir says as he grabs and pushes me out the front door of the market.

"You are a real coward, you know that?" says the young gentleman, standing there with an angry expression.

"Oh, am I now?" Nazzir starts walking toward him; I immediately intervene and jump in front of the unknown man.

"Sir, please do us both a favor and just leave."

Naz grabs my arm and pulls me back.

"Get off of me; you are hurting me!"

"Zadie, why are you always protecting the next man?"

"Nazzir, I didn't do anything. All I did was ask him to leave; why are you overreacting?"

"You know what, walk the fuck home."

"Nazzir, what do you mean?"

Nazzir storms out of the supermarket. I run after him.

He makes it to the car rather quickly, but I can't catch up with him.

I yell, "Nazzir, stop, where are you going? Why are you doing this to me? Naz, it is cold, it is just about to rain, and I don't have an umbrella. Please don't leave me."

While still running to the car, I just can't catch up. I stop and watch him peel off. I throw my shoe, hoping it'll reach the car, but it doesn't.

"You bastard!" I scream as I stand there, exasperated. "What are you looking at?" I spit aloud.

"I don't know you, but would you like me to take you home?"

"Take me home... You can't be serious; I don't know you. Maybe if you just went about your own business, this would not have happened." I'm trying to avoid his penetrating stare.

"It amazes me every day how my sisters do not know their own worth. Do you have any idea how strong and beautiful you are?" His puzzled eyes attempt to read my expression.

"You can seriously cut all that Sister Souljah shit out. It doesn't work with me."

"Miss, I have two younger sisters that I would kill for if a man were to ever lay hands on them. There is never anything that serious for a man to place his hands on a Queen. However, it was a pleasure meeting you; I wish it was under different circumstances. Good luck, and always remember that you are beautiful," he says as he makes his way back into the supermarket.

"Zadie," I say eagerly.

"Excuse me?" He about-faces.

"Zadie, my name is Zadie, as opposed to miss?" I state, barely able to lift my eyes from the ground.

"Don't do that," he says as he walks his way toward me. When he arrives, he softly grabs my chin, lifts my head, and gazes into my eyes.

"Don't ever feel intimidated to raise your head high, Queen." My intrigued unsettling expression is elevated as I step back from his grasp.

"I don't know you, sir, and I feel very uncomfortable this close to someone who didn't know my name but just a few seconds ago. I am going to call an Uber and head home. I appreciate your kindness." I take out my phone and request an Uber; thankfully, it'll be here in a jiffy.

"I didn't mean to disrespect you; I suppose I was caught in the moment; pretty asinine of me."

He shares a focused look into my eyes that is very intimidating, and again, I look to the ground.

"You are really tempting me to lift your head again," he says with an adorable smirk.

"But you are right, Zadie, you don't know me, but from what I just witnessed, I am the last person you need to be afraid of; however, I completely understand."

My, my, my he is one fine brother!

"Zadie, it looks like your ride is here. Have a safe night, and I mean a safe night. By the way, you have a beautiful name. Nice to meet you, Zadie, my name is Jayden. Jayden Carter. One last thing. If you ever need a catering service, please feel free to contact me."

I do grab his card, knowing very well he is trying to hit on me.

"Thank you; I may take you up on that offer."

WEEKS AFTER THE MARKET INCIDENT, my mind is absolutely made up. I can no longer take the abuse. I am leaving my husband.

After the initial time he abused me, I've opened a separate account and have been saving every penny. I also bought a cheap car that is currently in storage along with other necessities such as a first aid kit, wig to disguise myself, a disposable phone, and other items I'll need in case of an emergency. I officially think my husband has lost his mind; I will no longer sit around waiting on him to *kill me*.

Phone chimes:

Hey baby Z, I am going to be later than I thought. I will be home in a few more hours. We also have another meeting tomorrow night. So, I assume I will be late tomorrow as well. Can't wait to get home; see you soon.

See you whenever Naz

Well, I guess I have the night to myself —better yet…

Hey, Mike, are you available tomorrow? I have time.

Several minutes later, he responds.

You know I always have time for you. Just tell me when and where and I'll be there.

Great! I will leave class at 1 o'clock; I no longer have transportation; he took my car. Would it be an issue getting me from school?

No, no problem at all, Zadie, I'll be there at 12:45. Send me the address.

I stare at the ceiling for hours, trying to get some sleep. This has become my normal, as I have no idea of Naz's capabilities. I am also excited to see Mike tomorrow. It's been so long, and I miss his scent; he wears this cologne that melts me. Just the thought of being with him in a few hours is putting me to sleep. However, to speed up the process, I grab some sleeping pills from my nightstand.

CHAPTER NINETEEN

Traveling from Suffolk County to New York City for class is a very long, tedious trip without having a car. My backpack is definitely heavier than normal because I have tonight's outfit, shoes, purse, the whole bit.

Since I'm not sure if Naz placed any underlying spyware on my phone, I decided to leave it home. I am only able to email Mike while in class; I know my sister will try to reach out to me, so I went ahead and sent her an email to inform her that I left my phone home before she texts me.

I KEPT my outfit pretty simple, a casual black wrap-around fitted dress with red pumps and my clutch. Yet he still looks at me as if I am wearing the most expensive outfit.

There he is waiting for me as I walk out of my school, standing there wearing blue jeans, a nice long-sleeve button-down with a cardigan over the shirt. A simple smart casual style. As always, he is sharp, but his eyes seem vulnerable. He cups my face, leans in, and kisses me. This kiss is different, though. It is heartfelt, deep, and sensual. He kisses me like he…

"I miss you like crazy. It's been too long, Zadie."

… missed me… I have to pull back from him. Looking in his eyes, I say, "Many people know I'm married, Mike."

"Nah, I understand. So let's go someplace no one will know you."

He assists me into his wagon.

I open the driver door from the inside. He gets in and grabs my hand, dreaming into my eyes.

"I was so worried about you, Zadie. I couldn't wait to see you."

"I am doing okay, even under the circumstances."

"Look me in the eyes and tell me you're going to leave him, Zadie."

I look him in the eyes. "Mike, as much as you mean

to me, I'm not leaving my husband for you. I'm leaving my husband because it is best for me."

He nods in approval. "That's the fire that will make me fall deeper in love with you."

"Glad I got your support, Mike; now can we get out of here so we can be together? By the way, where are you taking me?"

"A nice location; it's about an hour from here, is that okay?"

"Yes, absolutely. I'm usually done with class at 6:30 on Tuesdays. Then you have to also add the two-hour travel time to get home with public transportation. So I have ample time."

"Sounds about right! I'll have you home by 11."

I go to sleep so peacefully while holding his hand. I haven't slept this easy in weeks.

We arrive at what seems to be a location in New Jersey.

"Where are we, Mike?"

"Come on; I'll show you." He wraps his arms around my waist and leads the way.

He takes me to a beautiful revitalized beachfront in New Jersey. The location is brimming with trendy specialty restaurants, shops, and oddities.

We also go to Liberty State Park, which has a wonderful view of the New York City skyline. We take a long walk on the footpath with really good conversation. We talk about everything. This is what a perfect date is all about: getting to know each other much better.

"Are you hungry, Zadie?"

"Actually, yes. I can eat."

"Let's head back so I can get you something to eat."

We pull into a luxury building parking lot off of Hudson Street in Manhattan, also known as SoHo, the trendiest as well as one of the most expensive places to live. I follow his lead and don't ask one question. We go into an elevator, and he presses button P11. I assume penthouse floor 11. The elevator doors open.

"Welcome to my home, Zadie."

His place is a completely stunning, masculine two-bedroom, two-bath home with a large view of the Manhattan skyline. At least ten-foot ceilings, walls of windows, and limed four-inch solid white oak floors with a grand walk-out terrace with skylights. The bedrooms offer a surplus of space to relax. The kitchen is huge, as you'll be able to entertain in style. The bathroom contains an oversized, limed white oak vanity, travertine slab countertops, deep soaking tub, and separate stall showers with frameless glass shower doors.

"Do you see yourself living here, Zadie?"

My head swings back so hard in his direction. "Was that a rhetorical question?"

"I guess that answers my question."

"This place is amazing, Mike! And you're not a drug dealer, correct?"

His smile is no longer visible. He sighs. "Don't ever ask me that again; you know the answer to that question."

"The family business, right?"

"This is not what I wish to talk about, Zadie. Let's go outside on the terrace."

The terrace is classy and elegant, with a complete makeup of deck tiles, tons of potted plants in the corners, lovely furniture, string lights, and rain curtains with a beautiful view located just outside the bedroom.

As I'm looking over the banister, he walks up behind me, places his arms around my waist, and holds my hand. "This can be all yours, just say the word."

I turn around and plant soft kisses on his lips. "I miss you. I miss your touch, your cologne, your muscular arms, and your beautiful eyes. I love your company and how I feel when I'm with you. God knows I haven't felt this safe in such a long time, but Mike, I'll need time to leave him, and I will. However, I need to figure things out on my own, maybe even get my own place and start a new life. I'd love to live in this beautiful place of yours, as living in Manhattan is a dream I've longed for my whole life. I just need to find myself. I've been with my husband since before college. I mean, you and I can be together, but right now, I can't think about moving in with you. I hope you understand."

"I admire your strength, Zadie; you impress me more and more each day. You drive me crazy too." We laugh.

"Let me feed my lady. Take a seat. I'll be back."

He isn't much of a cook, so he made a quick stop and bought a meal from a gourmet restaurant in Soho prior to coming home. He picked up lemon chicken, asparagus, and sweet plantains. He uses the outdoor grill to warm the food by candlelight. May I add he also bought flowers. Mike lays a spread on the granite table on the balcony. For dessert, we have raspberry sorbet. Even though he didn't cook, his presentation is on point. The best part is I still have several hours remaining.

At this time, we are just lounging on the terrace listening to Babyface, with no troubles in the world.

"Baby, I'm sorry to break us apart, but I have to take this call."

"Please, go right ahead."

I love this place; it has so much character. I am just

listening to the chattering from a distance. We are on the 11th floor, but you are still able to hear laughter from below.

Mike sounds like he's in a heated discussion with someone. I creep closer to listen in... *I told you about this over a week ago, have it here in 20 minutes you got that!?* He abruptly disconnects the call.

It is too late to sneak back, so I just stand there...

"Is everything okay?"

"Of course, why wouldn't it be?"

He takes me off my feet, my legs wrapped around his waist.

"I'm not done with dessert yet." I giggle softly as my body tingles, and my wetness grows. Each time he touches me, my body shakes.

He brings me into his master bedroom, unties my wrap dress, and as I unfasten my bra, he begins to trace his tongue around each of my nipples. He touches me like he loves me.

He leans my body up against the wall, kneels, and throws both legs over his shoulders, licking every inch of my inner thighs. Then he outlines his way up to eat my triangle. I am reaching for the ceiling to subdue my emotions and squeezing my breasts together. I can feel my body tense up, toes locked in place, breathing pattern becoming erratic; I am about to explode. He abruptly comes to a stop, looks at me, and grins.

"Not just yet."

I squeeze his ears and jokingly scream, "I hate you!"

He places my feet slowly onto the ground as I catch my balance. I grab his face and lick my sweet nectar off his lips. He turns me around as he places my hair in a ponytail.

"Kneel," he instructs.

He places his dick into my mouth, then begins to slowly move his waist and whirl, making love to my mouth. I devour every inch. He pulls my ponytail with pleasure. I sense he is about to detonate. He picks me up, throws me on the bed, flips me around, grabs my waist, and pulls me up. Now I am facing down with my ass up. He places a condom on his dick, turns my head to the side, and kisses me. He enters my pussy from behind, with circular strokes, slapping my ass cheeks. I arch my back, pushing my body deeper into him. He glides his manhood in and out of my pussy and kisses my mid-back, then my ass cheeks; he makes his way up, then begins to suck on my earlobe.

"Lie down."

I eagerly place my back down on the bed; we are now facing each other, sweating profusely.

"You love this, don't you?"

I nod in agreement. He kisses my nipples, then my navel. He grabs my legs and places them both behind my head. Once again, I feel his dick opening my pussy. This is too intense, a feeling of pain and pleasure. I am trying to back away.

"Uhhh, no, we don't do that."

He grabs me back in and continues to fuck me harder and harder. His dick is buried inside of me. I grab the nearby pillow and place it over my face to muffle my screams.

"You ready to come with me, baby?"

"Yes, yes, please!"

He gently places my legs down; we are now in a missionary position. He is looking directly into my eyes, kissing me and licking my chin. His tongue traces my collarbone, circling my nipples with his thumb. He is not moving, but his warm dick rests inside of me. I moan, breathing heavily, lips shaking, anxiously awaiting his next move. I surprisingly climax; we actually both come. I bury my head in his chest and laugh.

"Well, that was different."

"It was definitely different for the both of us, Zadie." He kisses my nose. "As much as I hate to say this, *we* need to shower, and I have to take you home."

"Yes, I'd like that."

Mike drops me off in the town before mine, which will allow my husband to witness the Uber drop-off. Mike follows the car to make sure I am safe and won't leave until I email him. Upon arriving home, I see that all the lights are on, which is odd. I scurry inside.

"ZADIE, why did you leave your phone at home!?"

"It was an accident, Naz; it won't happen again. I am sorry."

"Your sister is in the hospital; we've been trying to call you all day, then I realized your phone is home. Why would you do that?"

"WHAT? What do you mean she's in the hospital? Stop questioning me; just tell me what the fuck happened to my sister?" I say contemptuously; I have some balls! I am furiously worried; I don't care about anything at this time but my sister.

"Oscar was in a car accident. Let's go."

"OMG, was sis with him?"

"Nah, she's good. Let's go."

"I have to use the bathroom." I run to the bathroom in the study, email Mike, and tell him the situation. I can't wait for his response.

CHAPTER TWENTY

*Z*amora is sleeping on the hospital chair.

"Zamora!" We scurry toward her. She opens her eyes, getting up from the chair.

We embrace each other.

"I heard. Are you okay, are you hurt?" I canvass her body.

"No, I've been calling you all day, sis! I heard you left your phone home. Please don't do that again!"

"I sent you an email hours ago telling you I didn't have my phone."

"I didn't check my email."

"Oscar, is he okay? What happened?"

"The doctors are yet to update me. It happened so quick, Zadie. He left my place and called me using

Bluetooth as he normally does during his route home. Literally, only three to four blocks from me, all I heard were screams, Zadie, just screams."

She can't fight back the tears and can no longer stand; I am propping her up as much as I can. I guide her back to the chair and support her head in my arms while she weeps.

"I ran and ran, and I didn't even realize I was barefoot. Per witnesses, a minivan ran the light and hit him. His car was flipped over. I couldn't open his door, so I climbed through the back window. He was alive; Zadie. He told me he loved me for the first time. I can't lose him; I can't!"

There is nothing I can say at this time; I am in so much shock, so I just hold her. "I'm here, sis; I'm not going anywhere." She rests her head on my shoulder.

Looking over sis's head, my eyes widen, and my eyebrows frown. Mike is sitting several seats from us with a baseball cap and scarf covering half his face. I want to crack up laughing; he looks like an idiot. I don't know whether to be upset or flattered. I am assuming once he received my email, he just followed us here.

"Sis, you need to eat. I'm going to go to the vending machines to see what they have, okay?" She nods.

I signal Mike to follow me. Naz is relaxing on the sofa, not completely sleeping, but his eyes are closed.

The vending machines are just around the corner.

I jump and squeal as I feel a sting on my rear end. Mike slapped my ass. I chuckle. He pulls me to the side of the vending machines and embraces me with a hug and kiss.

"Baby, as much as I want you, I cannot do this right now. What on earth are you doing here!?"

"I know, sweetheart. I read your email; I had to follow you to make sure that you were okay. I'll leave, but first, just let me know how your sister is holding up."

"Not well. She is torn up, as she should be. I might sound terrible, but I am relieved she wasn't with him. I'd die if I lose her. Mike, let me get back to her. I will email you the moment I get home."

"I beg of you not to forget; it doesn't matter how late, you hit me up, iight?"

I grab a turkey sandwich and orange juice from the vending machine then head back her way.

"Hey, sorry to wake you, but you need to eat, sis." I hand her the meal.

"Thank you."

When I return from the bathroom, my sister is leaning on the doctor's shoulders, crying profusely. I roll my eyes to the ceiling. *This can't be good.*

"Zamora, what's going on?"

She immediately turns to cry on my shoulders. She is shaking and shivering. "He didn't make it, Zadie; he didn't make it. I just want to go, I can't wait for his family, this is just too much to bear." *Fuck*!

"Understood. Just come home with me. You can stay for as long as you need to."

She agrees.

Naz wakes up hearing the commotion. He comes to us, grabs Zamora, and gives me the keys to get the car.

ZAMORA HAS BEEN STAYING with us for three days, and on the third day, I am finally able to get her out of bed and into the shower. God knows that room smells like a dead animal.

She can't stand in the shower; she is too weak, so I draw a bath for her, assist with taking off her robe, and place her in the bath. As I turn to walk out of the bathroom, she says, "Sis, please stay with me."

"Of course, let me help you."

I grab the loofah and assist with washing her body and cleansing her hair.

"How does dinner sound tomorrow?"

"Yes, I don't see why not. I need to eat anyway."

"Great!" The conversation is very eerie, for obvious

reasons. She has to gradually get back to a normal life one way or another. She has yet to reach out to his mother and other family members, who have been calling her off the hook. I've answered a few of their calls. They seem to really like her and want her to be part of the funeral arrangements. She has to understand they lost their bother, child, uncle, etc. She isn't the only one that lost someone. I think it is time to let her know that.

"Sis, you really need to reach out to his family. They desperately need to speak to you."

"Why, though? I mean, we've only been dating for several months. I am nobody to them. He has many ex-girlfriends that lasted longer than me."

"But they are not you, honey; you were probably better than most of the ladies. Don't allow that negativity to cloud your better judgment; you are such an amazing woman. He knew it as well as his family."

"Give me one more day; I'll call them tomorrow, or maybe the day after. However, I will call them."

"Perfect. I'll leave and let you finish your bath. I'll check back in a few. Would you like a glass of wine?"

"Yes, please, and thank you."

I go into the kitchen grab a glass to pour the wine. Naz enters as well, standing behind me.

"Z, I've been meaning to ask. Where were you

coming from the night we went to the hospital? I checked your Uber account; there were no trips from the LIRR."

"Naz, leave me the fuck alone! My sister is going through a lot right now, I don't need your silly-ass questions!"

He roughly grabs my arm, pulling me close.

"If I find out, Zadie, I'll kill both of you, you understand?"

"Get your fucking hands off of me. Did you forget I didn't have my phone ALL day? So I was unable to call Uber. I logged into my account from school and scheduled a pick-up at the nearest location, Nazzir. Not every location schedules pick-ups, and that was the closest!" Even though it was a great lie, I give him a look that can kill, snatch my arms away from his tight hold, and then head back upstairs to my sister.

"Sorry!" he yells.

"Hey, sis, here you go. I bought some crackers as well."

"Thank you."

"I'll be back in 10 to help you get out."

I email Mike...

Hey. I miss you! Things are going pretty good here. Sis is finally coming around; we plan on going out for dinner tomorrow. I truly hope so; she really needs to eat. Anyway, baby, not sure if I'll be able to hit you back tonight, but if I can, I will. I promise!

This is simply not how I want the night to end, with my husband questioning me, especially since I have to sleep with him. My study doesn't have a bed, and sis is occupying the spare room.

Zamora makes her way out of the bathroom and into bed. She only had two crackers but finished the wine. I refill her glass.

I knock on the guest room door and enter. "Would you like another?" I hand her the glass of wine.

"Absolutely. Thank you so much for your hospitality. I know I must've been a thorn in your ass, but I appreciate everything that you and Naz have done for me."

"Sis, you'll never ever be a thorn in my ass. You are my world, and I love you to death, always remember that. Just as much as you should remember how special you were to Oscar, and his family needs you now. Please tell me that you'll give them a call tomorrow."

"Can I sleep on it?"

"Whatever you feel is best. Lie down and get some rest. I love you."

"Sis, maybe I'm asking for a lot, but do you mind staying with me tonight?"

"You are not asking for much, not even close. I'll shower and come lie with you in about 20."

I clean out the tub, burn some candles, pour bubbles, and get into my nice warm bath. Of course, I've brought my laptop to check my emails.

I am very thrilled that your sister is doing well. Thank you so much for the updates. Baby, please don't get upset. I have to head out of town for business for a few days. I'm also relocating from my current residence to Queens, much closer to my grandmother, as you know, she is very ill. I just want to get as close to her as possible. I am not sure how long this will be; however, I do know the moment that I am able to reach out to you, I will; but this is very important for myself as well as my family. I hope you can understand. I'm sorry I didn't inform you sooner. This absolutely sprung up on me overnight. email me as soon as you can before I leave.

My whole life just flashed. He responded to my previous email seven minutes ago; I hope that I am able to catch him, but I am trying to compute what I just read. *Several days, he doesn't know how long.* What in the world is going on here? I knew something was off; he's probably a drug dealer as I thought! Who just gets up and leaves!?

Ahh... I have tons of questions, Mike. Where are you going, what business do you have to conduct out of town? You barely provided any information; you are keeping me in limbo. How can I go on without seeing you for God knows how long who would do something like this!?

I am beyond livid right now; let me get out of this tub. I'm no longer in the mood. I decide to take the laptop with me.

My sister is sleeping by the time I arrive. I can do some schoolwork in the meantime and wait for his email.

Three am comes around and still no email from Mike ... I've sent him several emails between the hours of 10 and now but no response. I'll try to get some sleep now.

I remove the wine glass from my sister's hand, cover her with the sheets, and get into this California king bed. With the number of things that are on my mind, I just know I won't be able to go to sleep, so I decide to play some slow jams from my laptop that should put me to rest.

CHAPTER TWENTY ONE

"I'll just have the bisque soup."

"Sis, you must have more than that, please." We've made it to lunch—a simple diner near my home. We've made plans to head to Zamora's place after lunch to grab a few things she needs.

"Okay, I'll also have a side of fried scallops, is that okay, boss lady?"

"I see somebody's sarcasm is back… but that's fine, I approve."

Sis is done with her food, so I decide to shoot her the question…

"What do you think about giving his mother a call now?"

Her expression goes blank.

"If you are ready?"

She nods, grabs her phone from her purse, and dials out.

She's doing very well; I can partially hear his mother on the other end. Sis is mainly apologizing for going missing the last few days. His mother is very understanding. She agrees to meet her to discuss funeral arrangements. I whisper, "Tell her you'll offer to pay for the catering if they're having a repast."

She shakes her head no until I tell her I'll pay for it; Zamora offers the idea, and his mother gracefully agrees. Later in the week, they figure out a day to meet. The call ends.

"Zadie, he has a huge family, it's going to be expensive."

"Sis don't worry about it; I got you. This guy gave me his card; he owns a restaurant. I'll give him a call and check out his prices."

Lunch comes to an end. We arrive in Queens; I purposely took a different route to avoid driving down that same intersection that took his life. Upon entering her home, she isn't stable at all.

"I can smell him, Zadie."

She belligerently takes the sheets off her bed, throws them in the trash, then takes all of his clothes and does the same. He left a watch that she decides to keep.

After that episode, she goes outside to sit on the bench to compose herself. I follow, not saying anything at all.

"I think God doesn't love me. I finally made a change in my life, and he snatched it right away. I am trying to remain positive, but it's very hard. I changed so much of myself within these last few months because of your encouragement and Oscar; then boom, he snatched him clean away from me... He was great to me, Zadie, flawless, and all."

An incoming call interrupts the conversation. *His mother again.* I can't quite pick up what she is saying, but Zamora just keeps thanking her and crying. Then the seven-minute call ends.

"What happened?" I ask, then a strange look rises upon her face as she stares at me then back again at her phone.

"Oscar...." She pauses.

"Oscar what, sis? What happened?"

"Oscar left me eight thousand dollars to help open my ballet studio. This was declared in his will." My eyes widen, brimming with excitement.

"What did you say about God not loving you!?" I state sarcastically.

"Zamora, this is so exciting; it is such a major

come-up for you. This was what he wanted for you."
She begins to cry; I hold her hand.

"Sis, with the funds my husband and I gave you, as
well as Oscar's money, you'll be able to do so much,
from furnishing, remodeling, advertising, and anything
else you need to do in order to build your studio. Due to
the circumstances, I know it is difficult to wrap your
head around all of this; you take all the time you need
to grieve. However, this is such a huge deal for you! I
think we should have dinner tomorrow to celebrate; it'll
be great."

I am full of excitement, so I can't stay seated. I
stand there waiting for a reaction. She is understandably
emotionless and in shock. She stands and embraces me
with a hug.

"Thank you, sis, for being here, for being by my
side. He loved me; he really loved me. I can clearly see
that now. Thank you, Oscar, thank you so much," she
says as she looks up toward the sky with her hands in
prayer form. "Yes, I think dinner and drinks will be just
fine tomorrow."

"Sis, I will always be here for you through thick and
thin. Will you be coming back home with me?"

"I think I'll stay home tonight, sis, thank you. I
know you have a lot to do. I don't want to keep you. I
am fine, don't worry about me."

"Zamora, I don't mind staying; anything that Naz and I need done will get completed some other time."

"I am fine. Just get back home before traffic picks up; I love you so much, sis." She embraces me with a hug.

"I love you too, Zamora. If you need anything, and I mean anything, call me!"

As soon as I get into the house, I tear off my clothes, start my bath, head to my study, grab my laptop, and then get into the tub. I check my email—*nothing* from Mike. We've been talking for several months; he's never done anything like this.

Good evening Mike, just checking in on you; I haven't heard from you all day. At least let me know you are okay.

Naz enters the bathroom. I quickly minimize the email screen and restore my assignments.

"I didn't hear you come in, baby. You doing okay? How is sis?"

"We are doing well; thank you. You looked peaceful; I didn't wish to bother you."

"I made dinner. Come down when you are done."

I nod.

"I love you, baby Z; you know that, don't you?"

"Do you? With the way you've been treating me, it is very hard to tell."

He gives me an obscure look, leaves the bathroom, and closes the door without saying another word.

I just lost my damn appetite; guess I know where I'll be sleeping tonight.

Later that night, while watching TV, I slightly doze off. I hear Naz walking up the stairs, and I quickly turn around and act as if I was sleeping. He walks in, turns the TV off, and leaves.

Oh my, let me do one last thing before I lie down. I go into my purse and grab my wallet to email Jay for catering prices.

Good evening,

This is Zadie Baldamar, the young lady you met in the supermarket. I am emailing you to get a price quote for 100/150 guests for a post-funeral reception for my sister's boyfriend. Please follow up with me at your earliest convenience.

Thank you.

CHAPTER TWENTY TWO

As I am just about to walk out of the house, Naz asks…

"Are you eating with me this morning, baby? Just take a seat. We are going to eat breakfast together this morning."

Good lord. He holds up a finger and points to a chair. I slowly move toward the seat, sit down, then have breakfast.

I glance at Naz; he is staring at me while I am eating. He displays a sad expression on his face.

"This is hard for me to ask, even though I am sure I already know the answer. What made you sleep around on me, especially after everything we've been through?"

"I will not entertain your question; I would like to enjoy breakfast, thank you."

"You see, that is where you are wrong. You will answer my question." He throws my plate on the floor.

"Okay, fine! You want to know why? No penetration for years would make any woman go crazy; you didn't wish to use toys, barely even a vibrator. What did you expect? I lasted years, Naz, many years with no penetration, just masturbation. After I told you I had an affair, you changed up. But prior, you would eat my pussy once in a blue moon. What did you expect?"

I find no other way to confront his question…

"I honestly don't even feel like talking about this anymore, Naz. I have to go." While cleaning the floor and gathering my dishes to place in the dishwasher, I hear him settle in his chair. I glance at him, feeling slightly bad for what I said.

"Maybe we should see someone, Zadie, like a counselor."

"Maybe not; what will they do for us? Get your dick hard? I highly doubt that. Maybe you need to speak with someone in anger management and ask them how to not place hands on your damn wife! I need to go, Naz; we shall talk later, or maybe not."

As I begin to walk out of the kitchen heading toward the door, he tiptoes behind me, grabs my neck, and slams me up against the front door. He grabs my hair and forces my head back as he whispers in my ear, "You did this to us; you turned me into this monster, Zadie! How would you feel if I was only a few feet away from you fucking the next bitch in some back alleyway? How would you feel, Zadie, huh?"

I stand there in horror, telling myself over and over *I have to leave my husband,* the man I love with my life; I just never imagined he would snap so violently toward me.

"Naz, please let me go, please. You are hurting me."

He releases his hold, and I bolt out the door, run to my car, and fall into this crying mess. This is all my fault; my affair changed us forever. Maybe I should just agree and go to counseling, but I really need to walk away. I am extremely confused. I can't talk to my sister, as she is going through so much. Mike has yet to reach back out to me. I am just a complete hot mess… I have always been strong and determined; I must rely on that now.

While in my feelings, this lady walks past my car, and her head turns to look at me. That is my cue to drive.

Good Afternoon Mrs. Baldamar. Thanks for your interest in my service. Please provide a date and time you will able to discuss your inquiry. There are many factors in providing a quote. I have many options available. If you can, please provide your number. Thank you. Have a great day.

DIALING.........

"Hello, Mr. Carter, I just received your email; I figured to give you a call directly since your card had all of your pertinent information listed. Is now a good time to talk?"

After the call, we set up a time later in the day for all three of us to meet—Oscar's mother, me, and Jay to discuss the serving dishes. Unfortunately, Zamora is unable to make meeting.

The restaurant is called *Jay's Garnish* in downtown Brooklyn. This is surely a restaurant I have heard about; it has very good reviews on Google and Zagat. *Jay's Garnish* is tucked in, down three steps, as Ms. Mary and I enter the restaurant. There are about 13 to 15 white covered tables that made up the seating for the entire location. Candles are floating everywhere, and it has a modern environment. The dining area has pretty purple and black decorations, romantic lighting, and murals depicting various aspects of Africa, such as their royal wildlife, along with exotic locations of the vast continent. The restaurant showcases the rich culture and history of African people.

I request to speak with Jayden Carter and am directed to a table nestled in the back. The menu has a blend of many cultures from the agricultural south, Creole, northern, and western locations. The menu has pepper pot, collard greens, smoked haddock, buttermilk fried chicken, gumbo, Yankee baked beans, and more.

"Wow, this place is lovely. How did you hear about this location, Zadie?"

"I am pretty impressed as well. We met at a market in the east, not too far from my home. He handed me his business card. His name is Jayden Carter; I gather due to the name on the restaurant, this must be his spot."

"It is. Sorry to interrupt, good afternoon, ladies. I take it you are Mary. Zadie, good to see you again." He kisses the back of each of our hands.

"Please take a look over the menu. Anything you two order, I will spot the bill; excuse me, I am just arriving. I need to address a few things. I will be back momentarily."

Mary tilts her head to one side as if she wants to ask me a question.

"Is everything okay, Mary?" I ask.

"I damn near had a heart attack, girl, girl, girl; he didn't take his eyes off of you. He is very attractive. Are you sure nothing else is going on here?"

I blush. "Yes, I am absolutely positively sure nothing else is going on; this is my second time meeting him."

"I don't want to plant that seed, but he sure has it for you."

"He is a very attractive young man, but I am a married woman, Mary," I laugh and state jokingly.

"Excuse me, ladies; I was told to drop off a bottle of wine at this table."

"Thank you," we say in unison.

"Would you ladies like anything to eat?"

"Mary, would you like anything off the menu?"

"No, I'm not hungry. The wine is just fine," she says as she takes a sip.

"I'll actually take a Caesar salad and a glass of water, please."

The waitress goes to place the order.

Mary and I start talking about Oscar, what he loved, and how much he loved my sister. She is holding up surprisingly pretty well. She seems to be a very strong lady—admirable, I must say.

"Sorry, it took me longer than expected to get back to you two. I have my catering menu here. The prices are on the right side. So sorry for your loss, Mary. I'm sure it's not an easy time for you. I'm here to make it as comfortable as possible."

"Your smile is all I need, sir."

"Your wish is my command; please call me Jay, Mary…. Zadie, is everything all right? You seem pretty quiet," he says as he cups my hands with his own. For a moment, I can't move; every muscle in my body is tensed.

As some form of indication, Mary clears her throat and gives me a corner-eye look, which prompts me to release from his grasp. He rubs his forehead, staring directly into my eyes.

"I am just looking over the catering prices, thank you. Mary, I am sorry; I need to head to the little girl's room. I will be back shortly."

I walk away from the table as quickly as possible.

Leaning over the vanity, looking in the mirror, I tell myself, *Get a hold of yourself, Zadie; he just touched your hand.* I pull my makeup case out of my purse to freshen up. Instead of going back to the table, I allow Jayden and Mary to discuss the menu. There is really no need for me to be with them.

"Hi, gorgeous. What can I get for you today?" says a half-naked bartender. Wow, her body is flawless!

"Yes, can I have your body please?" We both laugh.

"I'll just take water with lemon, please, and thank you."

While drinking my water, I know I have to get back to the table, but from the look of things, they are pretty involved in a deep conversation.

"Would you like anything else or a refill?"

"No, thank you. I'm actually about to head back to my table."

"There you are, I was beginning to worry about your whereabouts," says Mary. "I actually need to head to the ladies' room myself. Are we just about done here, Jayden?"

"Yes. I have your check, and I've applied the discount. My staff will be there as stated on the contract; if there are any issues or delays, please don't hesitate to contact me."

Mary makes her way to the bathroom.

"I am sorry if my earlier gesture made you feel uncomfortable."

"Hey, don't worry about it, I'm fine, you're fine, we're fine."

He excuses himself from the dinner table. Turning back toward me, he says, "Zadie, please stay for dinner. You don't need to decide right now, but the invitation is open."

He is most certainly trying to lure me in with his burning eyes, pure white teeth, and perfect dimples, his six feet frame has a sexy muscular build, and his brown skin is slightly hidden beneath the shape-up and goatee. He is just... just.... so striking.

Mary arrives, snapping her fingers at me. "Earth to Zadie..." She comes back and sits down.

"Mary, sorry. I was looking for the waiter so we can pay our bill and head on out."

After a moment, Mary says, "The bill is already paid for. Did you forget that quickly, or you were just trying to figure out a lie to tell me?"

"I simply forgot, Mary, thank you for reminding me." I am, in fact, lying through my teeth. I'm sure she knows.

"Seems as if you were hawking at his sexy behind if you ask me."

I smile, sip my wine, and say nothing.

"Well, I think that wraps up our time here. I can't thank you enough, Zadie. You have helped tremendously, and his prices were great! Zamora actually overpaid; I will need to return a large sum when I see her in a few days."

"Please don't thank me; it was my pleasure. I can't imagine what you are going through. I am willing to help out as much as I can. I am going to order takeout, so we shall see in a few days."

We hug and part ways. I wave the waitress in my

direction. "Can I please place an order to go?"

"Absolutely. What would you like?"

I place my order and request another glass of water with lemon. I sit there, listening to music, waiting for my meal.

"I thought you were going to run out of here in a hurry, Zadie."

He touches my shoulder, then sits on the chair next to me.

"Do you mind?" He points to the bottle of wine on the table.

"It is yours, you paid for it, by all means," I say anxiously then look over my shoulder at the crowd. "I am actually waiting on my order to go," I mutter.

"Mary seems to be doing very well, on the contrary."

"We don't need to small talk, Jay; I am just waiting for my dinner to arrive," I say, exasperated.

He leans forward. "All right, Zadie, well, have a great night. I refuse to stay anywhere I am not wanted. Again, it was nice to see you."

"Thank you; it was great seeing you as well; thank you for everything you did for Mary today."

He nods, then exits the area. Thankfully, just moments later, my food arrives; I pay at the door then leave.

CHAPTER TWENTY THREE

"Hey, Naz, I'm sorry to wake you. I just wanted to inform you that Zamora is in the guestroom. Don't want you walking around naked in the morning. She didn't want to be alone tonight after the funeral, nor did she want to stay at her place."

"Okay, not an issue at all, baby Z."

"Oh, we also have tons of food in the fridge from what was left over at the repast. Good night."

It is a little past 11 pm. The funeral went longer than expected; however, everyone held up very well. Oscar's mother is such a great person. She made every single one of her son's guests remember his lovely grace. She definitely made his spirit felt throughout the entire funeral. Jay's staff and the food were spectacular; his staff was very efficient; they arrived on time and assisted everyone very well, and I believe not one person was disappointed with the food. I go to check on Zamora one last time, and thankfully, she is sound asleep. So I go to check my email before heading to bed.

Hi Mike, I'm going to assume you're no longer interested in me, trust me, I understand, especially with everything that I have going on. However, it's been several weeks, and at this point I just want to make sure you are okay. My email address will not change; I will keep checking for your emails periodically. However, at this time, I'm going to stop reaching out and fall back. I really hope that you and your family are doing very well. I'll talk to you some other time. Good Luck Mike.

"GOOD AFTERNOON, is Jayden Carter available at this time?"

"Sure, may I ask your name so that I can provide him with your information?"

"Zadie Baldamar."

"Thank you."

I decided to come down here and thank Jayden for his team's exceptional service, and to also apologize for the way I exhibited toxic behavior our last encounter.

Staring at his golden skin and muscular frame walking toward me intoxicates me...

"Good evening, Zadie, thank you for stopping by. How can I be of assistance?"

Awkwardness invades me. His voice is smooth; I bite my lip and clear my throat, as well as my thoughts. It takes some time, but I find the courage to speak as my voice cracks due to dehydration.

"Can we sit?" I point to the nearby table.

"Sure. Did everything go as planned yesterday, or did something go wrong?" he asks as he pulls out my chair.

"Your services were remarkable; your staff was extremely friendly and courteous as well as professional throughout. I just wanted to personally thank you for your staff's friendliness."

I keep moving uncontrollably, rubbing my knees with my hands, playing in my hair, twiddling my thumbs. I feel very uncomfortable for reasons unknown.

"What a load off. Thank you. That's great news. I thought something went terribly wrong."

"No, just the opposite." We sit silent for a moment.

I reposition myself on the chair. "About the other day, I apologize for being discourteous." I rest my hand beneath my chin and look at him. His hands are clasped in front of him. I take a deep breath. "I am going through a lot, and I've been edgy, snappy, and bitchy, again I am very sorry."

He leans forward, his eyebrows drawn together with intensity. "Your husband?"

I nod. "Is it that obvious?"

"Would you like something to eat or drink?"

"I'll stay for one martini, any flavor."

"Bear with me; I will be right back."

I loosen my limbs and sink into the chair. I am finally able to relax, and that martini will assist more with calming my nerves. While waiting for Jay to return, I see that the restaurant is pretty packed for the time of day. This must be the spot to come to for lunch.

Jayden walks back to the table with two martinis in his hands. "Very berry martini or peach pomegranate martini?"

"I'll try the peach pomegranate, please."

Again, my nerves start to resurface. *Relax, Zadie. Relax.* As a matter of fact, I take a large gulp, of the martini that'll hit me soon!

"I don't mean to pry—"

"No need for a disclaimer. Ask me whatever, Jay."

"Earlier, you said you were going through a lot with regard to your husband. Based on what I witnessed several months ago, why do you stay with him?"

I drain the glass and then inhale.

"Hey... Do you mind?" He attempts to cup my hands.

"No, it is fine."

"If it is that uncomfortable, we don't have to talk about it. Excuse me, Nannette, can we get two glasses of water and can I get another?" he says to one of his servers as he points to my empty martini.

"Thank you. This is not who I am, expressing my feelings to a stranger; I just have no one else to talk to."

"I am here to listen and not judge."

Some minutes pass, maybe two. I am able to get ahold of myself without feeling the need to cry. He sits across from me, waiting for me to gather my thoughts.

"I had an affair, I confessed and swore I wouldn't do it again, then months later he pretty much caught me red-handed, fucking the dude in the back of a club."

He listens intently.

"The same night at the club, he literally dragged me out by my hair. He never abused me the many years we've been together and married, but he was irate and lashed out. Originally, I kept telling myself it was my fault and I deserved it because of what I did. I mean, wouldn't any man react that way?"

I wait for his answer...

"Oh, I am sorry, you really want me to answer that question?"

I nod in agreement.

"Absolutely not, Zadie. However, proceed."

I close my eyes, but I can't withhold the tears. Nor do I care. I clear my throat. "It sounds ridiculous to say that I love him even though I've also had sexual relations with other men. My sister is more logical than I am; she believes marriage is just a word; it's a governmental contract that'll allow them to track us even more. She'll say people get married after being together for 10 years, then get a divorce after only three years of marriage. Sad how many marriages stay together because of what society and family members will think, or because of their kids. I always wondered why... Now here I am in the same boat, staying with my husband because of those three controlling words: *We are married.* Or better still, the sentence of *We need to fight for this marriage.* It sounds so ridiculous how people will put aside their happiness and their self-dignity because of that one controlling word: *marriage.* They even have reality shows based on marriage without even meeting the person. People like you and I will call that crazy, but it's their religion, culture, and their prerogative. Who are we to judge? If we look at their marriage as crazy, what makes ours better? Needless to say, my husband—aside from the abuse that recently started—is such a great man. He makes great money, he's my high school sweetheart, he caters to me, damn near never told me no; but something happened within his career…"

I draw back and inhale deeply. My lips are shaking, my heart rattling against my ribs. If my own discussion is making me uneasy, I guess my conversation would make anyone feel uncomfortable.

"Shall I continue?"

"I never hinted for you to stop."

"…Something happened with his career. He was injured, and doctors prescribed him with medication that hindered him from getting erections, which prompted my misconduct. The gentleman I am having an affair with—well, *had* an affair with, I actually thought of leaving my husband for. He was different, or so I assumed. But he was someone I thought would make me happy. I was wrong; it was a lesson learned. Not to say I'll stay with my husband because I know it will never be the same. But I need to start making myself happy." I am so dehydrated I have to take a sip of my water.

"I am so sorry. Here I am giving my whole life story to a stranger that I've known for only a few days. Your essence seems pure. However, I am sorry for the rant."

"Don't be. You had a lot on your mind, and I'm just here to listen with an open heart. So, to just confirm, you are no longer having affairs?"

"It has been almost two months since I've heard from him; he was going through a lot with a family member, and he needed to run out of town. Sadly, I never heard from him again. But he is in my thoughts daily. At one point I was reaching out to him weekly to no avail. So, eventually, I just cut my losses."

"His loss, Zadie, his loss. They say things happen for a reason. I strongly believe that. I also completely understand what you and your sister spoke of in reference to marriage. It is a permanent commitment that many people are not committed to; marriage is not meant to make you happy, as marriage doesn't do the work for you. I do not approve of affairs at all; yes, you were wrong, completely wrong. I'm going to be candid with you... I, too, am married. Just about a year ago, I found out my wife slept with my brother. Only two years into our marriage. I could've killed both of them. Just thinking about it makes me cringe. The only thing that I thought of was what my family would say if we get a divorce. After several months of constant agony, I just couldn't stand the thought of looking at her. I couldn't touch her for several months; we were two ships passing in the night. The sad part is, I was okay with that because I needed to figure out how we were going to part ways. I needed to make sure that our divorce would not put her in a bad state. That is just the person I am, I needed to depart this marriage knowing that she was okay. I refuse to be in a relationship *just because,* as you said, that word *marriage* is a killer. To continually be unhappy isn't the way a person should live. So trust me when I say I understand what you were talking about. Keep in mind, though, even after all that, I still never laid a finger on my wife. I grew up with the understanding that a man who put his hand on a woman, especially one who did not hit him first, is a coward. I refuse to put hands on any woman. There is just no excuse for it, regardless of what she might have done."

I'm still stuck on *she slept with my brother.* Holy shit… I sit there, aghast from what he just revealed. I know I'm trifling, but that's just scandalous. I am lost for words. I have absolutely nothing to say; he definitely dropped a bombshell about his personal life as well.

"Say something, Zadie."

"Oh, right, yeah, I'm sorry. I'm terribly appalled by

what you just told me. Your entire aura while telling me your story was so subtle. It isn't as if it happened years ago; it's very recent. You seem to be such a great guy. My husband is great as well. I know I was stupid for doing such a thing, but obviously something is missing, which prompted me to have an affair. But how are things with you and your brother?"

"We are working things out. It is extremely hard and heavy on both of us. You want to know something funny, their excuse was... alcohol, which I find completely unintelligent. However, things will never be the same between my brother and me. Obviously, he will always be my brother. I'd rather make amends with him and speak to him only once a year than make amends with someone I have to lie next to every night."

I can sense he is becoming very uncomfortable talking about this; I am beginning to hear his breathing.

I reach over to touch his hand to reassure him that all will be well.

"I am sorry. I know this is painful for both of us. How about this, let's change the subject."

"That's a great idea. So Zadie, you stated earlier that you have a sister. Is she younger, older, and most importantly, does she look like you?" We both chuckle.

"Hey, you are not single yet." He blushes and sheds light on his damn dimples. I smile so hard; I soften deep into his eyes as I peer at him. I'm sure he can read my thoughts.

"You are very attractive yourself, Jayden. But yes, I have a sister; her name is Zamora. She is my best friend. My world. She is about her shit, never met anyone so dedicated and loving as her. I always ask her for advice because she either has the remedy, plan, or statement for anyone's troubles. She is more of a hard worker than I'll ever be. Well, for now, until I finish school. Sadly, our parents were killed in a house fire; the only survivors were my sister and me. They made sure we made it out safe."

"I am so sorry to hear about that; I can't imagine what you two have been through. What are you studying?"

"I am currently at NYU, The Medical Residency Program."

"Get the heck out of here. Look at you, good work, sis! I'm impressed."

He is so full of excitement. "How much longer do you have remaining?"

"Slightly over one year."

"Wow, I feel like a big brother who is proud of his sister. Keep up the great work. I understand things are pretty tough at the home base right now, but always remain focused on you and your goals in life. Don't allow the free radicals to interfere with your plan, your motivation, and your dedication. This is huge; I am very delighted for you, Zadie."

He is brimming with enthusiasm.

"Thank you for being so positive and motivational. So this is your place, huh?" I observe his restaurant. "Very nice to see a brother in business."

"This old, rundown place—"

I quickly shut him down. "There's nothing old or rundown about your place. I have heard so many good things about *Jay's Garnish*. This is absolutely not an old or rundown spot; this is a popping spot. Don't be naïve. You know what it is."

"Much appreciated, Zadie. Will you like another refill?"

"Actually, it may be best that I head out."

"So soon?"

"Yes, there's too much going on in my life right now. I have studying to do, my sister needs help with her new location, and it is getting pretty late."

"I'll walk you to the exit."

"Oh, wait, let me pay for my drinks."

"You're kidding, right?" he says suddenly.

"Actually, no, I am not." I walk over to the hostess near the front door and pay the bill.

There he stands silently, tapping his fingernails on the hostess table.

"Will we see each other again and chop it up for a bit?" Jay says at the door.

"My sister and best friend and I always try to find new places to sit, sip, chat, and catch up. I'll absolutely suggest your spot for our next chill session."

"Okay, email me to let me know. I'll make arrangements to suit your needs here and at *Jay's Garnish.*"

CHAPTER TWENTY FOUR

Outside was a pale day, just as I was feeling. I folded and completed three sessions of marriage counseling with my husband. The sessions were so miserable! Most counselors have been divorced themselves and are biased. Most counseling is geared toward the way women communicate. Honestly, nothing has changed. He refuses to take anger management, so I decided to no longer continue counseling. He was miserable with my decision. However, I didn't care. He still frightens me any opportunity he gets; I am just not going for it.

When I come in, it is well after 10 pm. Of course, Naz is sitting in his chair in the living room watching boxing and yelling at the TV. I guess his meeting ended late. He is never up after 10. I signal and go upstairs.

"Zadie?" He stops me midway up the stairs. "You hungry? I have food in the fridge from the conference today."

"Oh, okay, well, it is just way too late to eat. You know I am trying to watch my figure." I laugh evilly.

"Guess you won't need to cook tomorrow since we have tons of food. Maybe even take a plate or two to your sister."

I proceed to walk up the stairs. I go into the bedroom and sit on my chair to read a few incoming texts and emails I couldn't get to while traveling. I purchased a personal tablet unbeknownst to Naz, just in case he downloaded some type of text tracker or GPS on the phone he purchased for me. I can reply to texts and emails without feeling obstructed, or without having any fear.

Email,

Subject line: Reminder that your Long Island Storage membership will be renewing soon

Body: Dear Zadie Baldamar,

This is a monthly reminder that your membership will be renewing soon. You will be charged 159.00 (plus any applicable taxes) for another month of Long Island Storage membership.

If you do not wish to continue your membership, please visit......

Group Chat:
Subject: Girls' night!

Zamora- Zadie, you went missing again?

Shelly- As always!

Zadie- I am here, you know, I have to drive home ALL the way from Manhattan to west bubble fuck.

Zamora- So ladies, I cannot make it to dinner tomorrow, how about the next day?

Shelly- As always!

Zamora – Shut up, Shelly!

Zadie- Nope, I am going to have to agree with Shelly on this one; you stay needing to reschedule some shit.

Zamora- (middle finger emoji) to the both of yall!

Shelly- Nah, she all bougie because he got her new place, she doesn't know the little people anymore!

Zadie- Shelly, again, you hit it on the nail!

Shelly- lol

Zamora- Inaccurate! Okay, okay, fine then. I

will make arrangements to come through tomorrow!

Zadie- YOU WILL NOT! We are just messing with you! We will go the day after.

Shelly- who is messing with her?

Shelly- lol I am just kidding, as well. Yeah, do you, girl! We are not tripping!

Zamora- Thanks, loves, well, I can't wait to see the both of you. It's been too long, and I am sure we have a lot of catching up to do! This spot you speak of so highly, better have great food, Zadie!

Zadie- Girls, you will NOT be disappointed! Trust me the food is tasty! Anyway loves, I am going to shut it down. I have a few things to do before I head to bed!! Have a great night!

Prior to closing the tablet, I have to make one last reply.

Jayden- lol. You don't seem interested in talking about your day. You shy away from the question and route it back to me. Understand that I am here for you.

Jay and I have been emailing for a few weeks. He's

seriously a cool dude. Even during our time chatting with one another, he never said anything distasteful or even remotely hinted he wanted more than just a great friendship. Well, I must admit there has been a little banter here and there, but nothing else.

He mentioned a few things that he and his wife used to do and how much he wishes things had not changed between them. He provided advice when I asked in reference to my husband and me. I would also give him advice, but he's adamant about walking out. I don't blame him, as he does not blame me for walking out.

I don't have the slightest idea of what I'd do if my husband slept with my sister. It is beyond a thought in my mind. My sister would ring the alarm if he ever approached her. But overall, my relationship with Jay is different. This is actually the only male friendship I've had during my marriage. It was always my sister, Mike, and Shelly. Several years ago, talking to other men was the furthest from my mind; at that time I loved my husband unconditionally, and yes, I still love him, just not how I used to. I regret what I did every day, which is why I'm still here trying to make amends one way or the other.

Zadie- I never pegged you as not being a good friend, I just don't want it to always be about me.

I'd love to continue to get to know who you are. Hopefully, I didn't wake you. I know it's pretty late; my drive from school is treacherous, especially with traffic. I apologize for the delayed response.

Even though it's been months since I've heard from Mike, I still check my email to see if he responded. I don't have any way of knowing how he's doing, or if he's back in town. I went to the bar twice, but I didn't see him. I even asked the bartender that knows him, but she hadn't seen him either. I gave up some time ago, but occasionally, I still look for him.

Jayden- Zadie Goodnight. Sorry to hear about traffic, but being that you are Miss bougie in the Hamptons, you forget how traveling into NYC can be. As for myself, I'm used to it lol. But, nah, you didn't wake me. I am just getting to my friend Cliff's crib for the night. I went to look at a few places to buy today pretty nice areas, and the amount is right up my alley. I try repeatedly, but I just can't stomach being at the house. Just to look at her boils my blood.

Zadie- bougie…. Bougie….. I currently do not have a comeback for that, but you better be prepared cuz I'm going to get in that ass when I see you! Lol. I seriously cannot imagine what you are going through; there is no way to return from that at all. I am surprised she even attempted to work on the marriage. LOL off the bat, I just would have known the marriage was over. There's no begging, no fixing, no reconciliation none of that. I would have arrived home, packed my bag, and left LOL. You never told me how you found out?

Jayden- I'd pay to see how you're going to get in this ass LOL! CARRY-ON! If you want to hear about that story... How about dinner next week?

Zadie- Put the money on the table, and I'll be happy to show you LOL talk is cheap, pay up lol. Next week..... sounds good, plus I haven't seen you in a few weeks; and I guess I have to see you in order to receive my moola. Lol

Jayden- first of all, Mrs. bougie nobody says moola anymore. Smh, I have to teach you a few things, don't I?

"I see you're still up," says Naz.

Fuck!! I completely forgot I was sitting in my bedroom doing all of this extra shit. I quickly slide the tablet into the crease of my chair; the laptop was already open on my lap. Naz doesn't know about the tablet. I hope he didn't notice.

"Yeah, just catching up on assignments. You know this time of year is just crazy…"

He walks toward me, kisses me on the forehead, and closes the laptop. He begins to kiss me on my cheek and neck. I guess he's in the mood… and I am not. We haven't touched each other in months… I just don't have it in me to touch a man that abuses me… We start kissing; the kiss actually feels pretty passionate. I grab his face and enjoy the kiss as well. Naz props his elbow on the granite side table to hold his balance while he gets on his knees. I slump on the couch; he places both of his hands under my thighs and cups my ass to pull me in closer as he feasts on my pussy with every stroke as if it is his last meal. My pussy is wet as hell. It's been a while since I have been pleased. He opens my legs wider; I close my eyes, my lips partially open as he covers my clit with his mouth.

"You taste so good." I feel his piercing tongue deep inside of me. How is he able to do that? Then he cleverly uses his fingers to accompany his tongue.

"Open your mouth!" he orders me. He then places his two fingers in my mouth. "See how good you taste."

I moan. I throw my head back and close my eyes with muffled moans. He sucks and massages my clit. I moan louder and louder. My restless abdomen presses harder against his face. I'm taking short breaths. I rear up with a loud cry of pleasure; I began to tense, squeezing my inner thighs on his ears. My climax is so powerful I break a nail squeezing on the armrest of my chair. He heads up to me with his mouth full, juice dripping down his chin. He leans over as he allows my juice to flow into my open mouth.

"I love you, baby Z. It doesn't matter what we go through, always remember that." Then he walks out.

Having sex with him absolutely clouds my judgment, which was why I never wanted to have sex under these circumstances. I just need to sleep. I take a quick shower, then head to bed.

CHAPTER TWENTY FIVE

"Now that was amazing!!" Zamora says as she practically licks the sauce off the plate. The girls and I have finally made it to *Jay's Garnish*. The place is packed, as expected on the weekend. According to one of his employees, he isn't here. I emailed him a few times today but haven't heard back. I assume he is just busy.

"I said you wouldn't be dissatisfied, sis."

"And you were not lying."

"Your sister is a foodie, all she does is eat bomb-ass food… I never doubted you, Zadie, you are, in fact, the person I will always go to when I ever need advice on food."

"Only food, huh, Shelly?"

"Well, no, amongst other shit," she says as we all start to laugh.

"Ladies...." The waitress arrives at our table. "I really hope you enjoyed your meal. That handsome young gentleman over there would like to offer this bottle."

"Who, chile?" Shelly literally props her breasts, licks her lips, and sways her gorgeous blond hair over her shoulder. She is very beautiful; and like my sister, they always attract men, but terrible ones that'll cheat and abuse them every chance they get. The difference between the two is that Shelly is always ready and willing to date. Sis, on the other hand, will go years without dating after a painful breakup.

"He *was* sitting at the bar." The waitress looks back at the bar, but I guess she is unable to locate the egotistic man."... When I see him again, I will let him know that you are seeking his attention."

"Thank you. I guess I will be taking an Uber tonight," Shelly says as she pops open the bottle of champagne.

"Please pour me a glass too, Shelly; I guess we all will be taking an Uber tonight."

"Not me, ladies," Zamora says. "I am sorry, but I just remembered I have this meeting tomorrow that I must get some rest for."

"Zamora, don't tell me you are leaving."

"I know, I know. Please forgive me. As you are aware, I am behind in work due to some punk breaking into my car. Then to add, I am doing so much with setting up my new location, I need to have things up and running in two weeks. Once that is done, y'all will have me back. I promise."

"Hey, more drinks for us right, Zadie?" Shelly raises her glass.

"Fine, Zamora. Text me when you get home, okay?"

"Come on, baby sis, don't give me attitude." I just wave her off...

"Zamora, you are not the only person in the world that has shit to do. I barely see you."

"I love you, sis, let's have our usual lunch Tuesday; I'll extend it for two hours. Okay?"

"I guess I have no choice but to accept your offer. Love you too. Drive safe."

"Zadie, don't let your sister screw up your night up. You know she is flaky from time to time, especially with loud music, sexy men, and drinks. Here, let me top that off for you," Shelly says as she refreshes my champagne.

"You are so right, Shelly. You know me, I get overly emotional from time to time. She is just so dull."

"I know, girl, but we love her nonetheless."

Phone pings.

You clean up nice …

Well, I don't want to toot my own horn but toot toot, where are you, Jay?

"Don't you ladies look ravishing tonight?" My back is toward the crowd. I am unable to see who is standing behind me, even though the scent is vaguely familiar. *Jay.*

"Thank you," we say in unison.

"Hey sexy, are you the fella that bought us this bottle?"

"No, I am just getting here. Hello, Zadie, happy to see you again."

"Glad to see you made it, Jay." He is eating me alive with his eyes. I don't blame him; I look dangerous tonight, with a curve-hugging black leather mini dress with a very deep V-neckline that practically makes it down to my navel. I feel the hairs on the back of my neck rise.

I break the stare, then clear my throat.

"Jay, I am so sorry that this is my best friend, Shelly. If you were only a few minutes early, you would've met my sister…"

"Shelly, it is a pleasure to make your acquaintance."

"The pleasure is mine, handsome." Shelly is so boisterous, and she is absolutely my alter ego; I only wish I had her gutsy ways!

He places his hand on my shoulder. "Did you ladies eat?"

"Where do you guys know each other from?" Shelly asks as she looks upon us with a huge question mark on her forehead.

"School! We went to the same school. I left to pursue my dream, which was to open this restaurant."

"Oh, this is your spot? Well, the plot thickens. So, what, y'all fucking as well? You know she is married, right?"

"SHELLY, are you kidding me? What is your issue? Why would you dare ask him that?"

"Just seems as if married women get all the right side pieces! While I am still trying to find my husband!"

"Shelly, I get it, you are probably drunk, but this is not the time nor the place for this childish shit."

"You are right, forgive me, I am going to the restroom. Pardon me." She storms away.

I aggressively stand up, turn my back to Jay, place my hands on my hips and grunt. "I am so sorry about her behavior."

"Come here..." he whispers as he grabs my hand and turns me to face him. "Dance with me?"

"Jay, I have two left feet, with alcohol in my system. It will not be a good look."

"I'll lead..."

"Shelly will be back any second."

"I'd rather you just say you don't want to."

As much as I want to dance with him, I just know it isn't the right idea, especially with Shelly here, this buzz I'm feeling, and how the both of us look. I don't want to give him the wrong impression, especially because I'm still in love with Mike and still confused about my husband. I don't need any more trials and tribulations in my life. Mike should be the last person on my mind right now, especially since he went MIA on me for months. But for some reason, I just can't shake him. Maybe it's because he was the first person I had an affair with, the first person I gave myself to the outside of my husband since we've been dating...

"Hey, hey, hey, sorry to interrupt you guys," says Shelly. "But the dude that bought the bottle for our table. I found him... He walked up to me as I was exiting the lavatory. Girl, we've been talking for the last 10 minutes. I quickly came over here to let you know that if you need me, I am at the bar."

"Look at that! Well, don't let me keep you. Do your thing, baby."

"Hey, my bad for snapping. I was tripping, girl."

"You're perfectly fine. Just don't head out without me, and ease up—"

"… On the booze…. Yes, I know, Mother." Shelly completes my sentence.

"Shut it; I'm not that bad. I'm just secure about my squad. My GPS is on. What about yours?"

"Ahh…"

She goes to her settings on her phone to turn on her GPS.

"…Yup, it's on."

Shelly kisses me on the forehead and goes about her business. Thankfully, we are in close proximity to each other, and I am able to view her sighting.

"Let's dance." I grab Jayden's hand and direct him to the dance floor.

I smile and start dancing, closing my eyes as I enjoy the music.

We are dancing as one. I feel a wave of awareness that tells me to stop, but I can't.

Unexpectedly the music gets louder, so the vibe between us becomes increasingly stimulating.

I don't want to look at him, but I open my eyes, and as I thought, I most certainly want him.

Our bodies are moving as if there were no one else in sight. My mouth waters as I eat up the sight of his melanin skin. My lips quiver with anticipation.

His body collides with mine, surging into me as I hungrily want him to kiss me.

He grips my waist; I can feel him breathing heavily. God, he feels good. The music stops—well, so I think. We stand there with a pulsating stare, both breathing in harmony.

I finally exhale. "Maybe we should head back to the table."

"That'd be a great idea," he abruptly states. Just a short walk to the table feels like an eternity as I don't want this moment to end, but we clearly need to shake out of it.

"Looks as if your friend Shelly is having a good time."

"She does, thankfully. But it is getting late; we should probably get going."

"Yeah, I am sure you have a lot to do in the morning, becoming a doctor and all."

"Oh, by the way, thank you for that."

"For what, Zadie?"

"Coming up with that amazing line about us going to school together. That was crafty, I didn't even think of that. You are impressive under pressure." I smile.

His observation drifts down my body as I sit there. I feel this outpouring of desire at the sudden fire in his eyes. I lower my eyelashes provocatively.

"Well, I am sure we'll see each other again pretty soon," I say as he positions himself in his seat, reaches over, and squeezes my hand.

"I know we will."

MY HOME IS QUIET; I have no idea where Naz went or if he is even coming back for the night.

Hey Chica, I am home; I had a great time tonight! I told shorty we would be back at that spot in the upcoming weeks. I am on the line with him now, so I will catch ya later; love you!

Thank you, Shelly. I am thrilled that you enjoyed yourself! You looked as if you were having a lot of fun! I am so happy! Love you too, baby girl! We will talk later! Enjoy your conversation 😊

CHAPTER TWENTY SIX

In the morning, I wake and lie quietly for a bit prior to getting ready for my workout. I am pretty tired from last night. I look beside me; Naz's side of the bed is as I left it. He never came home last night. Not implying he is seeing someone, but at least with my affairs, I made sure I came home. As I heard footsteps on the hardwood floors, I turned back around as if I was sleeping.

"Baby Z, are you up"?

I mumble something obscure.

"Baby, you hadn't responded to my emails nor any of my texts last night. I was worried. I was trying to inform you about my whereabouts; the crew went out. I drank a little too much and just crashed on the couch."

Oh shit! I have been so focused on my own secret

phone I forgot about the phone he bought for me. I must've left it in my other purse.

I turn around with a dreary, just-waking-up expression on my face.

"I am sorry, Naz, I was so busy. I honestly thought I replied. But I am glad you are home safe. You must be very tired."

"You bet I am; I am going to hit the shower."

I prop myself off the bed, open the window for some fresh air, and then head to my study to check my email, which I haven't checked in a few days. Maybe, just maybe, Mike finally hit me back. *27 emails what the heck*! Sadly, each and every email is from Naz....

I sit at my front door entrance, exasperated from my workout. I can smell Naz cooking something good. I guess he couldn't sleep.

Nah, my dude, put money where your mouth is, then we can talk. Naz is on the phone, chatting it up while cooking. So I do a gesture indicating I am heading to the shower.

Phone chimes:

Hey Queen, I hope you made it home safe last night.

Good morning Jayden. Yes, I did. May I say, Shelly had a great time last night.

My duty is to make sure my guests are well taken care of. What about you, you had a good time last night?

Yes, I did. I had a great time. ❤☐. Let's meet at our café later?

You beat me to the punch. I'd love that. What time?

After my studies. How's 4?

Sounds good.

I WALK over to the cash register and order my signature drink. "Can I get a large mocha here, please?" As I am ordering, I feel a hand gently caress the back of my arm. I turn around and see those heartbreaker dimples and those golden-brown eyes. He is looking as trim as always.

"Sorry, I'm late."

"We both were. You're fine."

"Here you go, miss. Your large mocha."

He places an order as well—a large black coffee with a couple of pastries.

I sit there looking pensively out of the window. Jay removes his shades.

"Are you okay?" He watches me for a moment as I gather my thoughts.

"Not really."

"What is going on?

"Just one of those days. I am overthinking. I thought I had everything sorted out. I thought I had the perfect career, husband, no children, ambition. Everything I have accomplished my father would be so thrilled about. I never thought I'd be here, in an abusive relationship, cheating on my husband. My mother is turning in her grave. My sister doesn't even know; it is way too embarrassing."

"Your sister doesn't know anything?"

"Nothing whatsoever. I don't know if she'll be more disappointed about the affair or the fact that I am still with an abusive man."

He looks up at me, but I just continue to rant. He is patient, doesn't judge, and listens very well.

Briefly, I glare at him, then smile temptingly. "You must think I am crazy."

"No, certainly not."

Gradually, we began seeing each other twice a week for pastries and coffee. It is a sigh of relief to just get away from all the turmoil within my home. I've damn near forgotten about Mike, but I still check my emails from time to time. Jay is someone I appreciate talking to, someone that makes me laugh. I consider him a really cool friend. I wonder if he feels the same…

ONE NIGHT we are watching the 10 o'clock news. We sit silently, not saying much to each other. Then…

"How would you feel if we renewed our marriage vows? We'll look for a nice small spot, not as big as the first time, anywhere you want. What you think?"

I guess many women would fly off the handle with excitement. Yet I sit there with a dead expression.

"Are you out of your fucking mind, Nazzir Baldamar?" I stand up from the sofa.

"I am still considering leaving yo ass for the way you laid hands on me. I can barely stand being in the same room with you. Have you not noticed, we are sitting in the same room, you on your recliner while I am sitting on the sofa alone? It has been like this for months. Do you really think a renewal will renew us? How silly does that sound!?"

He sits there, but quite suddenly, he strikes. "Damn Zadie, you didn't have to lash out like that, I just asked a question. I take it the answer is no!"

I am already moving toward the stairs to head to bed. He roughly grabs my arms.

"Don't fucking walk away from me while I am talking to you... Here I am trying to please your ungrateful trifling ass, and you turn your back on me?"

Before I know it, my back hits the stairs, while my knees are obstructing his swings. We are at it again! I roar out one good scream that startles him and loosens his hold; I quickly crawl up the stairs into my study and lock the door—he kicks the door off the hinges! I run to the window, propped against the sill to seek an escape. No luck. He charges at me like a bull in heat.

He grabs me by the neck, slams me up against the wall, and then throws me onto the bed. He is over me, like a bulldog slobbering.

"You just couldn't answer the question without all the extra mouth, huh? You just couldn't ride this shit along; you had to be difficult, didn't you? I couldn't even get *That was a nice gesture, honey, but let's keep working on us;* my whore-ass wife went straight off the cliff. You must still be fucking that nigga, aren't you?"

He then presses himself against me and begins to strangle me. After what feels like hours, I manage to kick him off me and run to the bathroom; I grab my phone, lock the door, and hide. He continues to kick the door and yell obscenities at me. I threaten that I'll call the cops if he continues.

"You'll call the police on me, Zadie, that's the foul shit you on?!"

He has some nerve, talking about being foul while I'm in a situation praying he doesn't kill me!

With a sigh, I shake my head; I should've left. I should've left months ago. I am shocked and confused with all that has happened. I just kept telling myself *He hurt me because he was passionate about me.* I was tugged by my hair, punched, kicked, you name it. I thought our love would've stood the test of time. The whole concept of *for better or worse* shouldn't mean remaining unhappy.

He stops banging on the door.

I hold my breath and watch through the keyhole. After hours of yelling and drinking, I believe he has fallen asleep. I go quietly to my study, grab a few clothes, my laptop, books, my tablet, my keys, and escape. I go to Manhattan and check in to a hotel, again telling myself I have to leave him.

I CAN'T SLEEP; I am tossing and turning all night. I need to talk to someone, but just didn't know who. Then again, I need to clear my mind alone. I decide to take a day or two away from class to get my thoughts together. I may need to call the cops to have them escort me to my home to gather my belongings. I cannot stay there; I must leave my husband once and for all.

The elevator doors open. I head downstairs to the lobby. "Good night," I state to the front desk clerk. "Is it too late for a glass of wine?" I can't sleep; might as well do something.

"Good night, ma'am, no, not at all. The bar is still open for about another two hours. Make this immediate left, and you'll see it."

"Thank you. Enjoy your night."

"Good night, I'd like to buy the Dom Pérignon, please."

"Sure, I'll be right with you."

"I am sorry, can I have a menu before you go?"

Anger races through my mind with the thought of Nazzir. Screw him; I am going to enjoy my wine tonight.

"I guess it is single ladies' night at the Park Lane Hotel," the lady sitting a few stools down from me states in a joking manner.

Returning her same energy, I say, "Seems like it, right?"

"Marissa, my name."

"Pleasure to meet you, Marissa. My name is Zadie."

"Zadie, that is beautiful and exotic. What does it mean?"

She is drop-dead gorgeous, very tall, with a seductive look, long dark hair, full lips and smooth beautiful dark skin that simply takes my breath away. Here I am, just getting my ass kicked by my husband, wearing two different color socks with flip flops on, definitely not impressive and most certainly not my style. I assumed no one would have been down here this time of night especially on a weeknight. Then again, I am staying at one of the best luxury hotels, the Park Lane Hotel in the Midtown Manhattan Business District, a 46-story hotel with panoramic views of legendary Central Park and the iconic New York City skyline. I should've assumed a few people would've been at the bar.

"It is an English name. Means princess. Zadie is a derivative of Sadie, which means princess and is also viewed to mean independent."

"Beautiful name for a beautiful lady. Where are you from?"

She moves her seat closer to me, and we sit for almost two hours, just chatting. She even spots my tab. I assertively tell her not to, but she insists. She has two little daughters; I believe her father is a very wealthy man. She went to Westminster College in Utah, then graduated from the University of Utah for communication. She seems simply wonderful.

"Is your husband also here at the hotel?" Says Marissa as she touches my knee.

"No, I left him home."

"Why did you travel so far from Long Island?"

"As you are aware, my school isn't too far from here," I say. "All I know is Manhattan; it is always the perfect place to go that is local."

Marissa nods. "I completely understand."

I'm drinking a little too much for my liking. Laughing way too hard and loudly, and I need my bed before my wobbly ass falls off this stool.

"Ladies, would you like another bottle or maybe another appetizer before I close out for the night?"

"Yes, another bottle of wine is just fine, Rodney." Why not? I am living it up tonight! No phone, no annoying husband, no sister, just a sweet night full of fun and laughter with a perfect looking stranger.

We go to her suite and converse all night. We talk about our upbringing and our future plans. We really dig deep into each other's life. I feel very comfortable with her, or maybe I am just very drunk. Either way, she has such a beautiful soul. We are silent for a while.

My hands are clasped tightly in my lap as I sit on the room sofa.

"To be honest with you, Marissa, it's been weighing heavy on my mind. I guess I just want to talk to someone about it."

"Of course, you can talk to me about anything, Zadie. What is it?"

She clears her throat, then sits next to me.

"I am leaving my husband because he abuses me every opportunity he can get."

"Oh my, you? Gosh, I would've never…. I am sorry to hear that. But yet I am glad that you decided to leave; he doesn't deserve a woman like you anyway."

"Phew, that took a lot to say again aloud; it is very hard to come to grips with. I never in a million years thought I'd be here, one of those ladies that gets abused by her husband. As they say, a fool for love is a fool for pain."

"Do you come here all the time when things happen between you two?"

"No, I just did tonight after he attacked me. I said enough is enough, and I snuck out."

"You think he'll come looking for you?"

"I have no idea, but I did try my best not to leave any breadcrumbs. He bought me a phone a few months back that I felt had a tracker on it. So I left that phone home. A few months back, I bought myself this phone without him knowing."

"Speaking of phones…" She grabs it.

"I just put my number in your phone and texted myself so that I can have yours."

"Thank you for doing that."

"Forget about him…Keep flipping him the bird, pack your shit, and begin a new life. You are beautiful, and you will find another mate rather quickly." She runs her fingers through my hair.

CHAPTER TWENTY SEVEN

W hen I wake up the next morning, the first thing I see is her beautiful smile next to me. She leans over and kisses me.

"Good morning, beautiful."

WHAT THE FUCK! I'm sure there's a comical look of confusion on my face.

"Are you okay, Zadie?"

I sprint off the bed, slightly dizzy, I guess from the hangover. She gets up to assist with keeping my balance... She guides me back to the bed and sits beside me.

"No, I am not okay. What happened last night?"

"We made love; you don't remember? You must've been pretty hammered." She giggles.

"Why do you think this is a laughing matter?" I say with haste.

"I am sorry, I didn't mean anything by it." She reciprocates my same attitude.

"My bad, Marissa, I am just confused. I am sure it was a beautiful night."

"It was, we enjoyed every moment. The memories will come back to you. We can make one more memory before I leave..."

"Leave?"

"Yeah, I have to catch my flight back to Utah. You don't remember anything much about last night, do you?"

"I guess I don't."

She leans in and starts kissing me gently. I start to tense uncomfortably. Mentally I imagine myself pushing her the fuck off of me, but I just can't produce that vision.

"Just breathe, lie back, and indulge," Marissa says as she begins kissing my breast, slowly making her way down to my inner thighs.

"I want to kiss you right there, is it okay?"

I begin shaking. This is so weird! Her tongue is moving very skillfully.

She kisses both of my thighs before running her

tongue toward my beauty. I clench my teeth to contain my groans.

Marissa's hands and plump tongue quickly run across my whole body. It seems as if she is in a rush as she wastes no time with preliminaries. I am deliriously engulfed in the satisfaction, and I can't even think straight. I say to myself, *Fuck it*. One hand cups her breast, and I start to gently rub the side of her face, then run my fingers through her beautiful hair. I rest my head back in a trance as she drinks my sweetness.

My legs become weak. I am thrusting my pelvis toward her finger. I watch as she sways her head in and out of my pussy.

"I can taste that you are enjoying yourself. I can see that you are as well." My slickness is all over the place. She places my legs over her shoulders. I start moaning and jerking erratically, grabbing her head, pushing her deeper into me. I can see her arm moving back and forth, and she hammers me with her fingers.

"Fuck!" I come in her mouth. My hot sugariness drips, and she licks every drop. She climbs my body and looks me in the eyes, kissing me.

"You won't forget that, right, Zadie?"

I think she just turned me the fuck out!

"No, I will not forget, Marissa. I hope you won't forget about me."

"Trust me, I won't," she says while getting dressed to leave.

"I have an odd feeling about this, Marissa. You are amazing, you literally just blew my mind, and now you are packing to leave. Is this normal behavior for you?"

"No, this is not normal behavior for me. Okay, yes, I've had relations with women, but not like this. Not a one-night stand. I felt so connected to you last night. Your frequency was so high. I enjoyed every part of you, mind and body; I felt your chakras were aligned; you name it, I felt you loud and clear."

She walks to me and holds my hands.

"I wish I could stay, but I have to get back home to my daughters. I know this is all confusing for you; eventually, you'll look back at this and laugh. When I come back into town, you will be the first person I will reach out to. Also, when I get into the taxi, I will text you my email address; please don't lose contact. And Zadie, please, I beg you, leave that son of a bitch. You deserve so much better. I must go now; my flight is leaving shortly. The room is yours until Tuesday. I had to cut my stay short, but I won't cancel the room, just so you can stay away from that bastard, and there won't be any breadcrumbs. Just take it easy on the incidentals."

We laugh.

"You have nothing to worry about. I am so speechless right now. Thank you so much. I will stay here for the next few days. Thank you again."

"No, thank you. We'll see each other again soon. But we'll talk all the time."

"Of course we will. Safe travels, Marissa.

"This is the beginning of something magnificent, Zadie, I can feel it."

"I can feel it too, Marissa."

We kiss and she exits the room. I've been staring at the door for the last several minutes. What the powerful fuck just happened... As much as I can't wrap my head around what transpired these last few hours, I can't help but cry.

Marissa_lopez23.@g.com. thinking of you badly.

I am still staring at the door.This is such an unsettling   feeling, Marissa.Zadiebaldamar@g.com

It is a new feeling; it will be unnerving for quite some time. But I am here to help you through it. We will help each other. Now, do me a favor. You still have enough time for complimentary breakfast. Go grab some fruits to replenish your body. Better to drink tea than coffee. Ask for Green tea, which has antioxidants that may reduce the fatigue feeling, then gain enough strength to shower. Okay?

.... Okay.

I will text you when I am about to board.

I do exactly as she advised. I feel much better. I bring an additional tea to my room, check out, and transfer my belongings to my new room. Upon entering, I realize that I hadn't noticed how amazing this suite is! It seems to be the executive park junior suite with a jacuzzi and has a clear view of Central Park from the 48th floor. I grab my laptop and place it on the charger prior to taking a nice bubble bath in the Jacuzzi. The candles flicker as the crackle of the flames put me in relax mode.

Marissa

Hey, I am here... How are you feeling now?

Picture sent (I sent her a picture of lower half-submerged under bubbles showing only one bare leg.)

lol, ahh I miss those thighs already.

omg, I am blushing.

You miss me?

Is it odd that I do?

No, not at all, I miss you too.

After reading her last message, I literally sink my whole body, head included, in the bottom of the tub for about two minutes. I am still in awe with the turns of events that occurred within these last few hours.

How long is your flight?

Nonstop 5 hours. I should land 3:15 your time. 5:15 GMT. I will hit you when I land. Don't overthink and spoil the flow. You will be okay. ttyl.

Safe travels. Ttys.

CHAPTER TWENTY EIGHT

I didn't realize it was after 2 pm already. I have been so involved in my studies. I put the pen down. It looks like it rained briefly. I turn my phone back on.

Jayden pinged

Hey hey hey!! Where you at? Been hitting you lady. Lunch, our normal time today, 4?

Shit, I never responded to him.

Jay!!! What is the deal!? So sorry about the delay. Ahhh, I am 10 min away; no class today, I took the day off. How far are you?

I hustle to put clothes on, awaiting his response. I

wasn't able to bring many clothes; Jay will finally become acquainted with the laidback Zadie look. I will have to pick up a few clothing and cosmetic items after lunch.

Still waiting for his response, I check my email.

Just school info and Naz, apologizing for his actions, usual shit! After many attempts to reach me, I guess his chest got pretty tight. He started to get upset and stated that he will find me and drag me through the streets again, and how he'll kill any dude I'm with—on and on!

Pardon the tardiness, I can meet you in 10 as well! See you shortly.

HE TURNS and looks at me with surprise. His eyes roam my body from head to toe. He stares so long until I break the stare.

"Zadie in a baseball hat. I think I like this look." I grin and blush so hard. He is already sitting at our common booth, and he already ordered my usual request.

"Yes, you are seeing another side of me. I am glad you like it." I have to focus so hard on pretending because of the pain and confusion that is buried inside of me.

"Zadie... Zadie? What is going on with you? You're drifting."

I snap out of my inner thoughts. "Jay, I left him; I finally left my husband." I don't want to hold back my thoughts anymore; it kills me. I just want to release any factors that are hindering my mental growth. It is not a good feeling to hold so much internally.

"Is your mind officially made up? How do you feel?"

"I feel good, I think."

"Did something happen yesterday?"

I nod. "He went crazy on me, Jay. I had to lock myself in the bathroom for hours." I start crying. He pulls out his chair and scoots in close to me. He places my head on his chest, caressing my shoulder.

"You are making the right decision, Zadie."

I raise my head and say, "I slept with one of the sexiest ladies I've ever met last night."

He starts choking on his pastry, staring at me with widened eyes.

"Whoa, whoa, whoa, Zadie! What in the world is going on here? Your last 24 hours were full of amusement, I see! How in the world did that happen?"

"Last night, after waiting in the bathroom for hours,

I grabbed what I was able to, then snuck out. I checked into The Park Lane Hotel. I was unable to sleep, so I went to the bar, and there she was. We kicked it; we even topped off two bottles of Dom Pérignon. I was so twisted last night. I woke up in a panic beside her, completely clueless as to what occurred.

"She gave me a synopsis of the night, but it is so cloudy. Like she spiked my drink. She didn't want me to forget the evening, so she coerced me into another session. I sat there; she just had her fun with me... This may all sound like some type of fairy tale or thriller, but I don't get down like that at all! Well, before yesterday. I have to tell you, Jay. She was breathtaking, and I can't stop thinking about her; her energy was/is vibrant. She might have put some type of spell on me! Funny, not funny. She had her room reserved for a few more days, and she told me I could stay. She was out here on business. She lives in Utah and went back home this morning, but we haven't stopped texting. Here, if you don't believe me, look, here."

I hand him my phone, and he surely looks. He is sitting there in amazement. He can't believe it any more than I did. Out of nowhere he starts laughing!

"Jay, this is not funny."

He keeps laughing. He can't stop. Now we are both laughing.

"This is deep, Zadie. You are a lady of many secrets."

"That seems to be my life."

He looks at me, carefully searching my face. "What are your plans this evening, Zadie?"

"Just more studying. I didn't go to class today; I needed to clear my mind. I may go tomorrow. I need to pick up a few things to wear; I wasn't able to grab much while running out. I may have to drive to NJ to withdraw cash because banks list the location of ATM withdrawals. I don't want to conduct any institutional business out here. I'd rather use cash than my credit card. I just don't want him to locate my whereabouts."

"Come on, let's go." Jay takes his final sip of coffee, grabs my hand, and leads the way. "We are taking my car."

We get into his car and drive to Bloomingdales on 3rd Ave.

"Here's my card. Get what you need. I'll wait for you right here."

"Jay, no, I can't accept this."

"You can, and you will unless you want him to find you. Just go, and don't take too long."

"Then can we go someplace cheaper, JCPenney's, or even Kohl's?"

"Zadie, do you want me to go shopping for you? I

am sure you wouldn't like that. Get an outfit for dinner tonight as well. Of course, after you study."

"Wow, Jay, I can't thank you enough. I appreciate this so much, Jay. I'll be back in a jiffy."

After an hour of shopping for the essentials, makeup, clothing etc. I am finally on the checkout line; Jay is going to kill me. I didn't think I'd take this long. I am exhausted. My lack of sleep is most certainly catching up to me.

Sorry I am late; I am safe and sound, my lady. How are you feeling? Marissa.

My body tingles.

Hi, don't worry about it. You're just getting home; I am sure you had a lot to do. I am doing much better now, just picking up some clothes.

Perfect, so glad you are feeling better. I couldn't stop thinking about you.

Likewise.

Maybe tomorrow we can talk for a few minutes?

Absolutely, I'd love that, Marissa.

Duty calls, we shall talk tomorrow. Have a great evening, my lady.

Have a good night, Marissa. Tomorrow! Just text me when you are available.

Upon running to the car, I cry out.

"I am sorry. I am so sorry." He hops out to assist with the bags.

"Don't be silly, Zadie, you were fairly quick. My counterpart would've been in there for about four hours."

"Thank you again, Jay. I just needed a few things to hold me over till I go back home."

"Back home?"

"Well, yes, I think I will have the police escort me to gather my belongings."

He starts to drive.

"Where will you go, what will you do?"

"Well, tomorrow I will go to my bank, then transfer funds. A few months ago, I opened a personal storage out east, not too far from my house. I have been loading that with many of my items in preparation for leaving: car, emergency food, etc."

"Resourceful, I see! I am proud of you."

"With this maniac, I have to be several steps ahead of him. Anyway, enough about my life. Where are we eating tonight?"

"You'll see. I'll pick you up at 7. Is that cool?"

"Yes, I will study for about two hours."

We finally make it to my car and part ways. I make it to the garage to park my car, then to the room to study.

———

HE ARRIVES LIKE CLOCKWORK. I have on this flirty style elegant hunter green floral lace dress that wraps around for a flattering fit and a dainty scalloped hem. This dress was absolutely figure-hugging with a contrast techno crepe and green pumps.

When I walk out of the hotel, his gaze is locked in on me. He is leaning on the passenger side door waiting for me to arrive. He eats me up with his stare, biting the corner of his lip. He reaches for my hand.

"Hi, Jay." As always, he looks mouthwatering.

"With everything you are going through, you look stunning. From the way you walk, your sway, your confidence, sassiness, and power. It is written all over you."

"Wow, I needed to hear that. I didn't want to possibly spoil the flow with lingering issues. Just hearing you say that helps me rebuild my confidence. Thank you!"

"You are more than welcome."

We enter the car and drive silently for a few minutes, then out of nowhere, I lose myself and start to cry. He pulls over to take care of me as he observes my tear-stained face.

"Zadie, look at me, look at me." He places his hand on my cheek and turns my face to his. "I understand you are going through a lot. But I need you to always smile for me. Look me in the eyes and smile for me."

I can't help but to smile.

"There we go, baby girl. Know your value, reward yourself; you came a long way. You need to look in the mirror more often. Not just look but talk to yourself as well. Talk positivity into your own eyes. Smile for me one more time." And there is another smile. "Are you ready to eat, cause I'm hungry." I blush, bow my head, and nod in agreement.

He lifts my head.

"You know I hate it when you look down in dismay."

"I am extremely sorry." I pat the tears off my face, trying to prevent my makeup from smudging. He narrows his eyes at me.

"One last thing, Zadie, stop apologizing. People often say they're sorry when they're feeling insecure. Force yourself to feel more self-assured."

CHAPTER TWENTY NINE

"Do you always look so serious when you're about to pay a bill?"

He stares at me for a few seconds. "You might be right. I'm trying to figure out the math for the tip in my head, so I must focus just a little bit."

"You know I too can pay sometimes."

"I'm going to ignore that comment."

While laughing… "No more alcohol for you. You're a mean drunk, Jay!"

The restaurant was pretty amazing. Every spot he takes me to, I am never disappointed with their entrées; the food is always on point—then again, he is a chef with exquisite taste.

"I'm going to call an Uber for us; I'll accompany

you to your hotel to make sure you are safe, use the restroom, then head to Cliff House. Is that cool?"

"Of course. I wasn't going to allow you to drive. I can drive, but you don't want me touching your precious car."

"Never! Let's go!"

I jokingly nudge him.

***

"YOU WERE NOT JOKING; this hotel is a beast. I always drive past it just like most hotels in Manhattan and never stay. Wow! Look at the view. This is amazing, a complete floor-to-ceiling view of Manhattan!"

We've finally made it back to my hotel room. He bought champagne from the bar. But I'm not drinking. After a night like last night, I definitely did not take one sip tonight.

Jay takes my hand and leads me to the sofa. He pops open the bottle of champagne and pours a glass, handing it to me.

"Jay, I am sure you noticed I didn't drink all night. I still can't tell you what happened last night. I never want to relive that moment again."

"Zadie, I get it, but this is different. One drink will not hurt." Holding up his glass, he says, "I would like you to shut off your mind. I propose a toast, to life, to you, and to new beginnings."

I smile. "To new beginnings." Then I take a sip.

"You see, a taste didn't kill you."

He is eying me curiously, as if he wants to say more. He runs his hand down his beard and swallows hard.

"All right, lady, get some rest. I requested my Uber ride. Café tomorrow our usual time?"

"You know it. If I'm running late due to class, I'll let you know."

He offers a faint smile as he begins walking toward the door. I lock the door behind him. *A nice bath would do right now.*

Oh shit! I run to the door.

"Jay, are you still on the floor?"

I'm not too far from the elevators; they are about a couple of doors down from the corridor.

"Yeah, what's up?"

He peeks around the corner. I wave for him to come back.

"Hey, sorry, Jay. One last thing before you go. Can you help me please?" I lift my hair, exposing the back of my dress to him. "Will you unzip me?"

"This is what you called me back here for? You couldn't find a hanger." We both chuckle.

"Jay, come on!"

"I am playing; I'll do it with pleasure."

A few seconds pass, yet he is just standing behind me... My eyes began to roam the room. *What is he doing?* Cool air passes over my uncovered skin, and he leans forward, pressing his lips softly on my shoulder, one kiss after another to the curve of my shoulders. As he traces his fingers down my arm, sending electricity down my spine, I turn around and face him. Our eyes hold a conversation without saying a word. He kisses the side of my face, then the bridge of my nose, his hazy eyes began to search mine. Tears drop to my face. He shakes his head no, and then he kisses my cheeks as the tears run down the side of my face. He is practically kissing each drip.

He whispers, "Should I stop, Zadie?"

"No," I say without hesitation.

He slowly backs me into the room, closes the door behind him, leans on the door, and pulls me in close, bracing my head on his chest as he inhales my vibration. He lifts my head, taking his time kissing my face.

"You're trembling."

"I am nervous. I've wanted this moment for so long, but I don't want it to damage what we—"

He places his finger to my lips, quieting me.

"Focus on me."

My dress puddles at my feet. I am standing there with my velvet and sheer lace bodice with matching panties and garter straps attached to my thigh-high stockings.

I stare at him as his gaze deepens into my body.

"You are stunning."

He unhooks the fastener of my bodice as I unbutton his pants.

"Take your panties off," he commands, pushing me over the edge. I place my thumbs on the elastic part of my panties and lower them, never breaking the stare.

He examines my body as his lips quiver. He steps toward me, closing the gap between us. He pulls me into him, flattening my breasts and holding me tight.

"Don't let me go."

"I have no intention of doing so, Zadie."

He picks me up. I yelp. He softly places me on the bed, then grabs a strawberry that the bartender provided complimentary for buying the champagne. He traces my lips with the chocolate-covered tip. He then caresses the side of my face and encloses a passionate kiss. As he continues to kiss me, I pull off his shirt, revealing his glowing skin.

He begins to trace his lips all over my body, circling around my breasts and nipples. He turns me on my stomach, his hands and tongue moving softly behind my neck and back. My breath becomes shorter. His kisses lower and begins to suck on my buttocks. Then the back of my thighs.

He turns me to face him. I open my mouth as our tongues meet; I pull him in closer to me as our kiss intensifies. I wrap my arms around his neck tighter, pulling him closer. His tongue caresses my hips and thighs and blows on my clitoris but only for a short time. He kneels on the bed, his *very* large fellow bulging through his boxers. I sit up and start kissing his chest and waistline. I pull his boxers down with my teeth, exposing his penis. He stops me, places the condom on, then lays me back down.

He pulls my legs up, and I wrap them around his waist, bringing him closer into me. I began to slowly grind on his member, anticipating when he will enter. Our kisses become more passionate. He enters…

"Uhhhh," I moan. While looking at me seductively, he is giving me everything. I am scratching his back as he makes love to me. I climb on top, thrusting up and down while grabbing and sucking my breasts. He moves me over to the side and lies behind me, sliding in and out of me intensely. My moans are becoming louder and shorter as I reach my climax. He flips me over, making love to me from behind and kissing my back with each motion. Once he comes, he lies in bed

and we both are catching our breath, staring lovingly at each other.

"You okay?"

I touch his face. "I feel great, Jay."

"Is something on your mind?"

I sigh. "I just don't want this to damage our friendship."

He scoops me into his arms. "It won't; I give you my word, Zadie."

We lie there for about an hour, just talking and laughing.

"I assume my Uber left."

"I am sure it did, and they billed you for the penalty."

"At this moment, that penalty means nothing."

"I am going to hop in the shower; I'll be back."

"Hurry back."

I sit on the bed and began applying lotion to my body, having just gotten out of the shower. Jay grabs the bottle and assists lotioning my body. He cups my breast while applying it. Circling my nipples, he begins to suck each of them. I pull his face up so I can feel his mouth on mine. He props my legs up on the bed to reenter me. I stop him; it's my turn. I grab him, sit him on the sofa, and run my tongue across his tattoo until I feel him go stiff. We make love my way this time.

"Do you have to leave?" Jay asks as I am getting ready for class the following morning.

"Yes, I missed yesterday. I shouldn't miss today. I am sorry. Will I see you at regular time today?"

"Absolutely."

After class, Shelly and I meet to grab something to eat. I have to reschedule lunch with Jay. I just need to get away from all the emotional mess that's been happening to me lately. I only have a few days left in the room. I have to figure out my next move sooner than later. Shelly is still kicking it with the guy she met at Jay's restaurant. I am so happy for her!

Upon arriving at the hotel, I go to check my email to see the bull Naz is talking about since this is the third night out of the house.

Surprisingly, he's only sent me two emails. The last email was at seven yesterday. It stated that he would finally take anger management class and is begging for me to come home. Well, it is a little too late!

Incoming email:

Subject line: Hey stranger

Hey, it's Mike. I know, I know!
It's been months. I went through

a lot. My Grandmother passed. I had to go overseas for work, then move to Queens. A lot transpired, and I know that's no excuse, but I needed to clear my mind. Please know that you haven't left my thoughts once. I think I am officially in love with you, Zadie. I feel terrible leaving you in the middle of such a turmoil time in your life; I should've been there. I just didn't know how. I read all of your emails and smiled each time. I hope you forgive me…. I am back, I got back several days ago, and I desperately would like to see you.

Email subject line: Re: Hey stranger

   FUCK YOU MIKE. YOU DON'T GET TO DO THIS TO ME!! YOU DON'T GET TO DO THIS!

I don't know what else to say. I was so close to just

forgetting about him! Then POW. He hits me up! Even though it sounds as if he has been through a lot, there are computers everywhere!

I deserve that. I am not even mad. I need you to understand; my mom/grandmother died in my arms, Zadie. The business was run by her husband, so we went overseas to make arrangements, deal with work, her death and the funeral. I need you to understand it wasn't easy for me. Can you understand that?

I am tremendously sorry for your loss. I know the feeling firsthand when you lose the most important person in your life. But, Mike, I lost my mind thinking and worrying about you. You could have emailed me a month ago; that may have been okay! But over 5 months? That's absurd! I really missed you. I was worried sick about you!

God, I miss you too, Zadie! I know I could've done a lot better. I admit that. I'll make it up to you, just tell me how?

Mike, you can't just pick up where you left off. This isn't that kind of party. I need reassurance that regardless of what is going on with you, you won't do this again?

I give you my word. That's all I have. Better yet, move in with me. I'll give you my keys, passcodes, cars, whatever, to ensure I won't go missing again, and if I have to make a run, you will then have full access to me. How about it?

T. XORÌ WILLIAMS

I smiled.... Well, I guess that'll be a start...

Are you ready for that type of commitment?

For you, Zadie, YES! These last few months have been all you. Talks of you, thoughts of you, songs of you, paintings that reminded me of you. Son and father discussions of you! It was all about you. To ensure your comfortability, I will do whatever I need to, but right now, I need to see you, hear your voice, anything.

DAMN IT! He melts my heart!

Things aren't the same anymore, Mike; things are different.

I don't care what you did in my absence. Fucked someone, whatever, I don't care. Unless.... Unless.... You decided to stay with your husband.... Or met someone else, is that the case?

No, Mike, that isn't the case at all... I waited for you... Well, sort of... Give me a call, Mike: 516.666.6588. We have a lot to talk about.

Mike and I talk on the phone till sunrise; we discuss everything. I refuse to hold anything internally. So I tell him about each of my sexual encounters. Where I am staying, how I officially left my husband etc. Also, I think I will take him up on that offer and move in with him. I am still debating on that, though.

CHAPTER THIRTY

The last few days have been pretty much a big blur. I haven't been home in 12 days. I checked out of Marissa's room and decided to change hotels; Marissa insisted that I should just relax and keep her room, but I just couldn't stay there because it was too expensive. I needed a standard hotel room. I was able to close out the account Naz had full access to and transferred the money into my personal account. Naz does email me daily, some good, but most of his emails are terrible.

The ringtone causes a disruption to my thoughts…

Zadie, it's been over a week since I've seen you. You begged for us not to change, but you're changing on me! Did you leave the hotel? I went to check on you, but someone else answered the room door.

I haven't been focused much on Jay since Mike came back. I'd love to see him, but he'll just confuse things a lot more! I haven't seen Mike either, but we do talk for hours each day. I need to handle my life first. After days of deliberation, I told Mike I'll move in with him. He was thrilled. He missed me and is dying to see me, but he is respecting my wishes.

As hard as it will be, sooner than later, I will have to let Jay know that we can no longer have sexual relations since Mike is back, and things are getting serious again. I wouldn't mind seeing his body one last time before moving on. I will see Jay later and explain everything.

Hey, Jay! Sorry, it is that time of year! Finals! Forgive me! Yes, I had to change hotels.

Zadie, you reprimanded someone for leaving and not reaching out to you, and here you are doing it to me! Don't make things odd.

You are so right! Again, I am sorry. I am meeting the girls tomorrow for lunch or dinner. How about the day after tomorrow? I'll text you the hotel as well as the room number; I'll leave the front desk with your name, to give you a key, what say you?

Yeah, okay Zadie, that sounds like a plan. Just hit me with the info.

I sure will. Hey, question... I need to provide you with my address just in case something goes wrong if I head to the house alone to collect my belongings. Will you be available in about an hour to chat?

I'll make time. Talk to you then.

I AM JUST GETTING BACK from class, heading into the garage of the hotel to park.

"You think I wouldn't find you, Zadie?" He yanks my head back so hard I am sure I lost some of my hair. He throws me onto my car, repeatedly beating me. I am finally able to see who was attacking me.

"Naz, stop!" I yell, trying to block his hits.

"You fucking bitch! You out here fucking dudes in this hotel!" He drags me off the car and onto the ground. He hits me a few more times, and I lie there crying in a bawling mess, trying to hide my face to avoid visible bruising. I scream very loudly, then I remembered I have a security alarm on my key chain. I blast it. It is so loud, it also pierces my ears! He runs off. I crawl to the elevators and make my way up to my floor. I crawl my way into the corridor of my hotel. I sit in the hallway for a few minutes to figure out what the hell just happened. How did he find me? I wonder if he has a GPS on my car, or maybe the change of accounts listed my location. I knew I should've gone to NJ! And again, I need to change to another hotel.

I finally make my way to the room. I immediately take off my clothes and deep-soak in the tub for about two hours. I practically fall asleep in the tub.

Thankfully my body isn't too sore; however, my right shoulder is killing me. I went to gather a bag of ice with hopes it'll assist with the healing, and it isn't broken. By nightfall, I've catered my shoulder for several hours while doing assignments. The pain is much better; it isn't healed, but there is definitely an improvement.

THE NEXT DAY, I guess I slept on my shoulder; the pain seems inflamed upon wakening. After lunch with the girls, I changed hotels and am now staying at the Trump Hotel in Soho. Even though I am not sure if he had a GPS in my car, to be safe, I've decided to use a taxi service and keep my car parked in a lot. I will head home to pack my shit in three days' time...

Jay, my husband found me! Will you be able to meet me at the Trump Hotel at 730 tomorrow?
 Hi Zadie, yea. That time works for me...

EPILOGUE

For what it's worth, I never thought I would want someone with such dire urgency as I do right now; no symphony compares to what I'm feeling at this present time.

Waiting by the windowpane listening to Sade's "No Ordinary Love" in the dark for a man I've longed for weeks to be with. The high tide of the world has been keeping us apart, but thankfully that has subsided.

Repeatedly I've told myself I shouldn't be here; I should just walk away. But yet being with him in his arms feels just right. It's where I find my safe haven, my home away from home.

I am patiently waiting for him at the Trump Hotel in Manhattan's SoHo district.

SoHo is one of the most commonly known areas in

New York City. The neighborhood is known for its artistic legacy, boutiques, and nightlife. We always wanted to try the hotel's luxury Hammams, Moroccan, Turkish spa treatment and head to the pool deck and have a cocktail in a private cabana. However, we can't enjoy the nightlife due to our unfortunate circumstances.

Even though we are unable to take pleasure in the hotel amenities, just being in each other's presence is quite all right.

I am staring outside New York City, and the sights are miraculous. I am surrounded by Manhattan's landmarks and historic sites such as the Hudson River, Midtown Manhattan, the Empire State Building, and the East River bridges. The sight is a wonderful blend of old and new; it is a delightful city, relaxed and fun.

I AM NOT much of an emotional person. However, waiting anxiously and nervously for this man, I just can't help myself. I am becoming increasingly emotional.

Hearing the thunder rumble and watching the raindrops fall, I press my forehead up against the window. Just the thought of soon to be lying beside this man marked by great beauty named Jayden Carter is nearly pushing me over the edge. Hmmm, I can feel his sweet kisses all over my body. For crying out loud, I smell this man in my dreams.

SUDDENLY, while in deep thought, I am startled by his muscled arms being wrapped around my waist. I inhale as if my life depended on it. He is here.

I slowly maneuver my head to the right, providing him with more room to kiss gently on my neck. My breathing pattern begins to deepen as I continue to endure his sweet kisses. I moan quietly.

This moment is endless.

I place my hand on the back of his neck and began to slowly gyrate on his manhood. He whispers in my ear in his raspy seductive voice, "How have you been, Zadie?" Before I am able to answer, he turns me around, looking intensely into my eyes.

"I've missed you so much, baby."

"I've missed you just as much, Jayden."

"You look good tonight."

"I try. Thank you." I'm blushing as if I was a twelve-year-old schoolgirl. He always knows the right things to say.

"Well, you seem to do a phenomenal job for only trying."

I am gazing into his gorgeous brown eyes, which melt me completely.

He softly kisses my forehead and inhales deeply. As he removes my cashmere shawl, I wince as if I was in pain or distress. Without delay, he steps back, observes my bruised shoulder, clenches his jawbone, and sighs.

"Let me guess; he did this to you?"

"Jayden, I really don't wish to—"

He silences me by placing his finger over my lips.

"We don't have to talk about it. Don't say another word."

By his increased heart rate and respiration, I can tell he is agitated, but I completely understand.

He places his hand on my lower back, pulling me in close. We then indulge in a soft, passionate kiss while caressing each other amorously. His hand slowly moves up my back toward my shoulder, and I flinch again. Thank God, this time, he doesn't notice. I couldn't bear to see his displeased expression again.

I immediately grab his hand and guide him to the other end of the penthouse suite that is surrounded by open curtain floor-to-ceiling windows.

We are on the 40th floor overlooking the beautiful Hudson River, no one in sight but just the two of us.

While walking to the other end of the room, he stops abruptly, embracing me tightly, my back to his front, planting soft kisses on my nape. At this point, I can feel his full-fledged erection; oh my, I can taste him already. He unexpectedly lets go of me, and I stagger.

While he walks into the kitchen, I begin to wonder what he is going to do. But I continue walking to the other side of the suite yet again, gazing out the window.

He's behind me.

Upon his arrival, he places my hands on the window, gently holds my waist, and begins to place delicate kisses on my neck. He raises my black sundress, revealing my bare behind. He continues to kiss me, one kiss after another, passionately massaging my braless breasts, circling my nipples with his fingers.

I begin to pant.

Jayden removes his hand from teasing my breast, then inserts an ice cube into my mouth. Oh gosh! It is only ice, but holy cow, it tastes like heaven. Jayden then opens my legs by using his foot. He places an ice cube in his mouth, then down my lower back; the ice begins to melt down the crevice of my behind.

With force, he turns me around; now my back is to the window. He drops to his knees, places another ice cube into his mouth, grabs my hips, and thrusts both legs over his shoulders. Swirling the ice in between my thighs, I gently whisper, "I've missed you much."

I am now taking short, fast, shallow breaths, rubbing my hands vigorously through his hair. He teases my love box by gracefully blowing cold air on it from the ice that is melting delightfully in his mouth.

While he's kissing my inner thighs, I begin to shiver with anticipation.

Climbing back to his feet, he miraculously takes off my dress as well. My legs are shaky but planted back onto the floor.

He stands in front of me, searching my eyes. He grabs my chin and embraces me with a soft kiss, while his other hand skillfully plays with my kitten. My bottom lip begins to quiver, and I just can't take this anymore. "Jay, I need you inside of me."

Without hesitation, Jayden turns me around. But he doesn't cross the threshold just yet. He begins to massage and place tender kisses on my bruised shoulder. I close my eyes to relish this moment. Before I know it, he is inside of me, forcefully having me from behind. He quickly ejects himself from inside of me, turns me around, and then wraps my legs over his waist. Now we are kissing each other ever so hungrily.

He carries me over to the chair. I am now astride him, moving up and down, thrusting myself onto him. I see that he is beginning to tense by the vein in the center of his forehead. So I began to smother his head in between my breasts, on my toes moving faster and faster, teasing the tip of his magic wand, and then back down the shaft. I do this repeatedly as I can't stop, then again, I really don't want to. Moments later, we climax simultaneously; we are breathless holding each other.

Then, out of nowhere, we start laughing like children. "I see we were eager," he says, still chuckling.

"Well, Jayden, it's been several long excruciating weeks. What did you expect?" We start to laugh again.

This is the moment that I love, the moment when we are away from our outside troubles embracing each other's laughter, love, and company. During my time with Jayden, I try not to think about life outside of him. I endure every moment spent with Jayden as if it's my last. Fairly often, the thought runs through my mind. The thought that Jayden Carter was the man I married.

T. Xorí Williams was born in Brooklyn, New York City. Xorí began writing woman inspirational quotes to friends and family, who often asked, *"When are you going to write a book?"* She finally wrote her own novel, inspired by Sister Souljah, Teri Woods, Donald Goines, Zane, James Patterson, Nora Roberts, Twilight, and the E. L. James series. While working two jobs and still attending school, Xorí began writing, completing her first manuscript in 2017. Xorí has developed an ability to alter many projects at once, researching one book while outlining another. Xorí then decided to self-publish her first novel online. From an early age, she always dreamt of writing stories that readers will fall in love with, and that dream has come true.

Please check out my other sites:

http://www.naturallylovelkinks.com

Made in the USA
Middletown, DE
06 June 2022

66752148R00156